To Lindy, Thank you for all you do!

The Quest

by

David R. Carney

"The Quest" is a travel and historical fiction adventure story, set in the 1950's about a teenager whose father was proclaimed Missing in Action in Korea and posthumously awarded the Silver Star for bravery. After losing his father and finding himself homeless the highly resourceful teenager then lives in the Arizona desert, and later shines shoes in Chicago.

When he learns an evil step father's plans to sell him into slavery, he stows away on a ship, panhandles in France, and then slips across the Iron Curtain Russian border to help set up a secret network delivering much needed medical supplies to Gypsies, all while wanting to return to his girlfriend in Rattlesnake Cove, Alabama.

Excitement, travel, and history throughout the book as Danny struggles to take control of his life.

1

Published by:

David R. Carney
NightSky Publishing
124 Timberwind Drive
New Market, AL 35761

Email: carney50@mchsi.com
Orders: www.NightSkyPublishing.com
Telephone: 256-652-2460

Printed in the United States of America

Cover design by Mrs. Ellen Hunter. Thank you, Ellen!!

Thank you, Mrs. Kellie Hicks, for your wonderful critique to see if my words made sense. You kept me awake many nights struggling to figure out how to correct the multitude of errors you found. Your many suggestions were incredibly constructive. Your help made this book so much better. I am very grateful to you.

Credits

Writing a book, especially an adventure historical fiction novel, is a huge undertaking. I did an enormous amount of research to make sure my dates and details were correct. However to do it right is an effort, and collaboration of many people is necessary.

My very first and most important supporter was my wife, **Judy (Marilyn Judith) Carney**, an accomplished author herself. We spent endless hours discussing what should be said in every conversation throughout the book and so many smaller details that help give the book credibility. This book would not have been possible without Judy's help. Thank you to **Sarah Zimmerman,** who just might be the funniest person alive (she claims to be a touch crazy also – in humor) for all her great support and encouragement.

The one question I kept asking everybody was does this make sense. Is this exciting enough?

One of my biggest supporters was my sister, **Elaine Holley**. She couldn't wait to read each page as I wrote it. My son, **Michael Carney** and my daughter, **Lydia Birk** were major supporters.

Others included my friends, retired **U.S. Army Lieutenant Colonel Marc Spencer and his wife, Donata**. They gave great ideas about Russia's Iron Curtain. **Retired Command Sgt Major John Perry and his wife, Brenda**, were incredibly supportive as they have been for many years now. **Retired Chief Warrant Officer Wayne Grimes and his wife, Shane**, contributed to lengthy discussions. Their young teenagers **Owen and Eden**

were very interested also.

Thank you to beautiful sweet cousin, **Dr. Kelly Araujo**, an awesome psychologist who works for a Veterans Administration hospital with military veterans. Kelly suggested the theme for this book - "taking control of your life." And that's what Danny is trying to do throughout the book.

Clifton B. Peppers, I thought of you the entire time I was writing this book. I understand how you want to get out and see the world. But above all you want to make a meaningful contribution. I know how much you have studied religion. Perhaps this story of a young man who kept struggling against all odds will help inspire you. In this story Danny kept seeing the work of God every where he turned. I am sure you will also. Good luck to you and God speed on your personal quest.

Chad Hinton of C and H Computer Repair in Meridianville, Alabama kept my computer running virus free throughout the writing experience.

Thank you to **Al Visone**, friend for over fifty years, for helping me with the Italian version of the Lord's Prayer.

Many people have asked if this is a bio. No, it is not. However, I did draw from my experiences traveling around the world and my many years traveling and living in Europe to give the book the many minute details that establish credibility and excitement. Most of my experiences I don't share, but I do draw ideas from them.

I give to my many supporters all the credit for the hoped-for success of this book. I reserve to myself all the errors for they are surely mine.

Table of Contents

Title Page	1
Publisher's Page..	2
Credits	3
1, Bad Memories, Tucson, Arizona, May, 1955	6
2, In the Truck - headed west	12
3. In the Tucson Desert	15
4. Dad's Family, Rattlesnake Cove, Alabama.....	18
5. The Lord's Day in Rattlesnake Cove	32
6. RattleSnake Church Service	39
7. On The Way to Chicago	52
8. Shining Shoes In Chicago, Illinois	57
9. Danny Learns To Speak Greek	66
10. A Close Call With Kidnappers	89
11. Gypsy Camp in Marseille, France	111
12. Panhandling in Paris, France	121
13. Slipping Across the Russian Border	146
14. Gypsy Camp Behind Russian Iron Border	173
15. Back to Marseille and America	186
Deep in the Bowels of Washington, D.C.	203
About The Author	205

Chapter 1

Bad Memories
Tucson, Arizona, May, 1955

I felt a sharp pain in my side and heard a command to get up hissed in my ear. I smelled the stale smell of smoke and beer and realized that Buford was kicking at me with the toe of his boot. "Get up, boy, and don't make no noise. Get in the back of that truck outside and don't turn on no lights." He commanded.

Here we go again. Another fast get-away in the dark of night. Buford drunk again and yelling at me as usual. Wonder where we're headed this time? Guess it doesn't matter. They don't want me and I'm just in the way, I thought.

The only clothes that I owned were in a pile beside my pallet on the floor. I rolled up the pallet, pulled on my clothes and grabbed my canvas bag that holds my only possessions.

Buford pushed me toward the door, "Get a move on. We gotta get outta here, pronto!" I saw that Mom was already in the truck and looking nervous. I jumped into the bed of the truck and pulled the dirty blankets around me. It was going to be another long, bumpy ride to who knows where.

There was nothing to do but hold on to the side of the truck to keep from being jolted out - and think. As usual, my mind wandered back to my dad and then to that awful day when we were told he had been killed.

I remember it so well. I was ten years old. My daddy was one of the last people killed in Korea. At the memorial service everybody gathered around me and hugged me and made a fuss about how sorry they were. Memorial service!! They didn't even bring his body back from Korea. Those people had no memories of my dad. I had memories. I remembered all those times we went fishing, to ball games, and movies, and walking hand-in-hand to the corner store, just Dad and me.

I'll never forget that military officer standing up in front of the church, reading, in a deep voice, "On behalf of Dwight David  Eisenhower, the President of the United States, the Silver Star is awarded to Sergeant Daniel R. Carmichael for heroism and for saving the lives of four fellow soldiers." Then he placed the medal on a folded U.S. flag and knelt right in front of my mother, my brothers, and me and said, "On behalf of the president and the United States Army, this flag is presented to the wife of Sergeant Carmichael."

Mom's face never changed. Not one tear. But me, I couldn't keep the tears from pouring down my cheeks.

At the time I thought most of them didn't really care. They were just glad it wasn't one of their own family. The preacher said Daddy had saved some soldier's lives. Then he said we would

all go to our home in the sky some day. I was at home until daddy died. This was all so horribly wrong. Suddenly I got so angry at all of them that I jumped up and ran out the back door of the church, down to the bridge to my and Daddy's favorite fishing hole. I hid under the bridge for three days, fishing with the line and pin I always kept on me and the flint dad gave me to build a fire. Then the police found me. They gave me the choice between jail or home. I chose home.

When I walked in the door the first thing Mom said was, "This is your new daddy. His name is Buford." I stood there quietly, trying to take it in, then I asked, "Where are my brothers?" Buford said "They've moved off. The people wouldn't take you. Now you go get out there in that truck. We're going to Arizona. There's nothing for us here in Tennessee."

Mom cowered behind the door while this big, ugly, smelly, drunk ordered me about in my own home. And it's only been three days since the Memorial Service, I thought. I could tell right then I was going to be on my own. I looked around the rooms that had been my home for as long as I could remember. My gaze settled on my daddy's flag, medal, and picture stuffed in the garbage can. Yes, nobody cared. I rescued them from the trash and placed them in my canvas fishing bag which had pockets for the picture and medal, my knife and some fishing line and hooks. I placed the flag in the bottom of the bag. The flag represented my entire life up to this time. Daddy had given me my knife. My most valuable and treasured possession. I often held it in my hand and remembered.

"I'm taking my daddy's flag. You never cared about him anyway. You wait, someday I'll be Sergeant Daniel R. Carmichael, Jr. and I'll be a good man too, just like him," I proclaimed to closed ears.

Sad Memories

Daddy was such a good man. He worked every day at the cotton mill as a spinner. Thirteen hours a day and six days a week. It was hard work and he was always so tired. Daddy was tall and handsome in his overalls.

Somehow he found time to take me fishing after church on Sunday afternoons. He always said "Sunday is the Lord's day and fishing is like the Lord's work. He fishes for men, but we fish for food. Let's go fishing!" Sometimes we even cooked our fish over an open fire, right there by the riverbank. They say Cherokee Indians lived along our river bank. I did find an arrowhead one time. We'd stay up all night with Daddy telling me about the old times.

Daddy told me stories about our background while we were fishing. It was like a family history lesson. "Family legend has it that just after the Civil War eight Carmichael brothers jumped ship and swam ashore in Charleston. They wouldn't let them get off the boat with everyone else. Said too many Irish here already."

Well, I didn't know about any of that stuff, but I loved hearing it over and over. Daddy said there used to be signs in all the stores up north that said "NINA." "No Irish Need Apply," he said.

He told me our Irish ancestors were Clan chiefs and very noble people who fell on hard times. But when they arrived in the United States our Irish ancestors had been branded with a reputation as thieves and of heavy drinkers, he said.

"In Ireland the English treated them awful and even stole all their food, under armed guard. They sent their ships and soldiers and loaded up all the potatoes and made the Irish starve." Daddy said. The Irish depended on their potato crop to feed themselves so no wonder they drank so much. But it turned out that what really happened is when they got to this country they proved to be hard workers and would accept any job. And then before you knew it, they became police chiefs and city councilmen and got other important jobs.

Daddy told me over and over, "Don't ever let anybody tell you that you have no value. Your ancestors were all noble chiefs and great leaders. Some day you will be one also."

Daddy told me about the Battle of Athens, Tennessee that happened just after he returned from War. "Some local criminals had taken over our town and were trying the steal the election. So our veterans all got together, stole guns from the armory, and demanded the ballot boxes be brought out and publicly counted. The sheriff armed 200 deputies and dared them to try to get to those ballot boxes. When an African American was shot that was enough. Daddy and his buddies had liberated Europe, so they knew how to act and what to do. They wanted our home town back. When we started throwing dynamite it was all over. The sheriff and his men feared for their lives and gave up. They had our home town back. Athens, Tennessee belonged to the people again."

The last time I went fishing with Daddy he gave me his canvas fishing bag. He told me, "Son, in this bag you have my trusty knife and flint to start a fire, you have fishing line, and you have hooks. My pride, though, is my harmonica. Your grandpa in Rattlesnake Cove, down in Alabama, gave it to me. You keep playing it just like I taught you. You will always be able to take care of yourself with the things in this bag.

"Danny, I have to leave again, our country needs me to go fight in Korea. They've called me back to war. Just a little battle they say. When my country calls, I have to go because I'm a soldier. That's what we do." Daddy put his strong arm around my shoulders, "So, I want you to keep this bag for me, no matter what, because I will be back, and we will go fishing again. Did you know I made this bag myself? Made it from an old army bag that soldiers carry their clothes in; it's called a duffel bag. See that "US" on the side? That stands for us - you and me. Daddy smiled a big smile.

Danny, you are the oldest of my boys and I am sure you will grow up to be a good man. A man that everybody admires and wants to be like. You make me very proud. We walked home hand-in-hand. My heart was broken that he had to go away and Daddy knew it. He kept squeezing my hand. I could tell he was sad, too.

After Daddy left, Mama started drinking and laying out at night almost from the day he left. She told me she was lonesome. She brought a lot of men home with her and she told us they were our uncles. I never knew I had so many uncles.

There was just me and my little brothers. Then one day there was only me. My little brothers were gone.

Chapter 2

In the Truck - headed west

The five days travel to Arizona in the back of that old truck was a nightmare. Baked by the sun and wind in the day time, I huddled in my blankets during the freezing nights. Always thirsty. Always hungry.

Buford had no money. We'd stop at a filling station and Buford would order us, "Stay in the truck." He'd then put gas in and then he would pull out fast, without paying, before the law showed up or somebody came out with a gun. At times I wished they would. Then this nightmare would be over.

Other times he'd order us, again, "Stay in the truck" and he'd run inside a food store and steal food. He was very tricky about where we would stop to steal. Always at a state line. Then we'd just drive across the line and they wouldn't be able to follow us. That's what happened in Louisiana and Mississippi. This was all so wrong and I had no idea how to change it. I did not want to be there. I wanted to get away, however I could.

Well, we stayed in Tucson, Arizona almost two years. We started out living on Ajo Way in a cheap one bedroom adobe house. I slept in the living room on a pallet. There was no sofa. In fact there was nothing. We were barely existing.

Then we moved and kept moving. We'd move to a new house and then after we went for two three months without paying rent we moved again. Since we always lived in the poorest neighborhoods I went to the same school the whole time. Mom was working as a waitress somewhere. She continued drinking, more and more.

Buford was gone a lot. Sometimes he'd have handfuls of money. Most times he had nothing and we had no food. I would eat at a Mexican friend's house. His mama was round and jolly with a pretty face and black hair streaked with grey. They didn't have much but she always made me feel welcome there. She even gave me some hand-me-down clothes from her older boys. I learned all about tacos and tamales.

I think Buford did a lot of illegal stuff and then he'd turn around and gamble it all away. He must have taken all Mom's money too, because she didn't buy us much of anything to eat. They never talked and I never saw any money. I was just kinda there, mostly on my own. My neighbor friends all talked about stealing stuff all the time. I know they were all just trying to get by. But I didn't want to be any part of it. And I am sure Buford was doing something illegal.

I always tried to make the best of everything, though. While we were in Tucson, I made friends who took me camping and taught me desert survival skills. The Indians, even the Apaches, had thrived in the desert for over a thousand years. The desert can be your friend. I learned a lot and started to feel at home again, even sleeping on that pallet, always with my daddy's picture next to me. I had my friends and my school and I loved the desert.

I joined the Boy Scouts and came to understand what an incredibly good organization it is for young people. It seemed I went everywhere and did all sorts of fun things. I went on camp-outs way up in the mountains with the Scouts and that's where I learned even more about desert survival. I learned how to make campfires. I learned which parts of a cactus are edible and I learned to watch out for scorpions and snakes.

Tucson, as rough as it was, nevertheless was becoming home. Maybe I was destined to live my life sleeping on a pallet and having thieves for friends. I didn't seem to be much good for anything.

That is until that late night when Buford started kicking me to get up. No idea why we were leaving. I know Buford had been stealing cars and robbing stores. Maybe the rent was due. Maybe the law was after him. I had never seen him so scared before. Maybe some bad men were after him.

Chapter 3

In the Tucson Arizona Desert

So we headed out to the desert to Saguaro National park, about 15 miles outside Tucson. You know it. Only place in the world where those big cactus with arms grow. For the next three months or so we lived under a canvas stretched between two small bushes. Buford was always going off some-where. He was gone at night and would return in the morning, only to sleep all day. Some mornings he'd bring back food. Most times he'd bring back nothing, except for the beer. There was always beer. Occasionally I heard him mention the border to Mom. I think he was running something across the border. Sometimes I heard drugs mentioned. Others times I heard people mentioned. Whatever it was I knew my life was in danger and I wanted no part of it.

Thanks to my friends and the Boy Scouts I had learned how to

kill and cook small wildlife. Once I even got a bobcat. I learned that you can cut a plug out of the cactus and it was pretty good. Some of the cactus flowers tasted really good. We ate well in the desert. There was never a problem finding water. Springs and streams everywhere. I became very self sufficient. The fruit at the top of the saguaro cactus was pretty good, I called them dessert. The cacti were so tall that I needed a stick to knock them down, though.

I learned all about rattlesnakes. They were everywhere.

First you gotta kill 'em; pretty easy if you're careful. What I usually did was pin the head to the ground with a forked stick. Then, very carefully I'd use my knife to cut the head from the body. I've heard that they can still bite even after the head is cut off and it's dead. I usually buried the head for safety sake.

Then I'd use my daddy's knife to cut a slit in its underside along the length of the snake and peel the skin back like a collar. Best to have two people to skin it because it wiggles so much, even when it's dead.

Then I'd peel the skin all the way off towards its tail, reach inside to remove the intestines and other internal organs.

Then you cook it. There are lots of different ways to cook it and lots of seasonings you can use, I learned. But I didn't have any of that. So I'd just put it on a stick above the fire and roasted it.

In fact most all the small animals were cooked the same way. You just removed the head, the innards, and the feet (when necessary), skin it, cut it into parts and roast it over the fire.

When it rained Mom and I would huddle together under the canvas. There could be terrible lightning storms in the desert. Buford was always gone so I had to be brave for Mom.

To my surprise I had found another home. It was my desert. This is where I belonged, or so I thought. Then my bubble burst.

I knew something was wrong when he pulled up in that old run down truck and he banged the truck door hard.

Chapter 4

Dad's Family
Rattlesnake Cove, Alabama

B oy, we're taking you to the bus station. You're going to
Alabama to live with your grandparents. Where we're
going they don't have room for you."

No idea how he paid for the ticket. I figured he probably made
some good money the night before and hadn't gambled it away
yet. "Thrown out of another home. Can't even live in the desert!"

I don't think Buford ever knew my name. It was always "Boy."
Here I go again. Does anybody anywhere care about me?

Six days on a bus to
Alabama. I hadn't had
money in so long that I
had forgotten what it
looked like. So weak
from hunger I got sick
and passed out. A nice
lady on the bus gave me water and a little of her sandwich.

All my life, it seems, some of my best friends were those people whose names I never knew. Most people are there to help, I learned. But not always.

That was such a long bus ride. I couldn't understand why it went to so many places before it got to my grandparents in Rattlesnake Cove, Alabama; Phoenix, Albuquerque, Dallas, New Orleans, Knoxville. Such long days and nights.

I missed a connection in Albuquerque and those bus station benches were really hard to sleep on. I got lucky and found a dollar bill, now I could eat. There were long layovers in Dallas and New Orleans. People left their newspapers and sometimes books, so I read some to pass the time.

Somebody was always offering to share their funny smelling cigarettes with me. That stuff smelled awful. And those bottles in brown paper sacks. I knew what that stuff was. Buford carried his liquor that way. "So the law won't get you," he said. I was leery of everybody the entire trip. Something was very wrong here; the people, everything. So hungry. So thirsty. Then I discovered food in garbage cans outside the restaurants when we stopped. From then on that's how I ate..

Bus driver tells me "Boy, we don't have a bus stop in Rattlesnake Cove. We just stop on the side of the road. So you'll have to stay awake and let me know."

"Boy"? I wondered if he was kin to Buford.

I spent my 12th birthday between Phoenix and New Orleans.

Daniel R. Carmichael Junior's new home.

After President Andrew Jackson signed the Indian Removal Act in 1830 people started moving into what used to be the Indian lands. Some of them found a very peaceful place on the side of a river in a cove between two mountains in the foothills of the Appalachians. They slowly invited family and friends to join them in their little piece of what they called heaven.

In 1955 Rattlesnake Cove was a very poor community; few telephones; no electricity; no running water; no paved roads. Just a little church and a general store with a sprinkling of farm houses. No locks on the doors because people couldn't afford the locks and everyone knew nobody had anything worth stealing anyway.

Everybody farmed small row crops and prayed they raised enough to carry them through winter.

They did have a post office after folks got together and petitioned the U.S. Postmaster for mail service. When they had to come up with a name somebody said "let's name it Rattlesnake Cove." For lack of a better name it stuck.

Grandpa and Grandma were there to meet me with their wagon hitched up to a pair of mules.

"Come over here and let me look at you, Danny. You're growing up to be such a handsome young man. You're the spittin' image of your daddy. Let me hug you," Grandma said. Before I could answer she pulled me close in a big hug.

"I'm glad to see you too, Grandma, but you're squeezing me to death!" I laughed.

"Son," Grandpa told me, "we are so glad you came to be with us. Let's go to your new home and we'll have lots of long talks. We've got years to catch up on."

I was finally at home. And somehow I became 'son' again. Life was really good. They even knew my name - 'Danny.'

"Danny, we just live a couple miles from here. We've got you a big pot of rabbit stew waiting on us. You'll be fat as a tick once she gets some of her good cooking in you. We ain't got much. We're as poor as church mice, but we're sure gonna pour the love on you. We're just as happy as a pig in mud to have you here," Grandpa said, with a big smile on his face. Then he busted out singing.

"Grandpa, you're singing 'Danny Boy.' That was Daddy's favorite song. He sang it to me all the time."

"And well he should, Son. That's part of why we named you Danny. You see, that was my daddy's name and his daddy before that. But I'll tell you more about my grandparents when we get home. Right now just sit back and look around as we go home.

"That's Preacher Wilburn's house over yonder. He's a good man, but he'll give you the dickens if you miss church. Look down on that side of the road at the creek.

See that grassy spot twixt the two oak trees? That's where your daddy and I always went fishing. Do you like to fish?"

"Fish? Heck yes, my daddy and I went all the time. Daddy told me that going fishin' is almost like going to church"

"Son, it was me that taught your daddy to fish," Grandpa replied. "you'd better not let the preacher hear you say anything about not going to church. Around here we go fishing after church."

"Grandpa, why is this place named Rattlesnake Cove?"

"Don't you worry about that now, Son. Just don't go around those big boulders all along side of the road and up the mountain. And watch your step everywhere you go. But, there's lots of time for me to teach you all about your new home. Here we are, Son. Take a look around"

Danny looked about the small wood frame house that had seen better days. The front porch with two rocking chairs and smoke slowly drifting from the chimney gave Danny a cozy feeling.

"I hope you don't mind helping your grandmother and me around our home. We're both all stove-up with arthritis and can barely get around," Grandpa told me.

"Grandpa, I'm here to help with whatever you need. After all, this is going to be my home too. And thank you so much for letting me come live with you."

"Our home is very simple. It's a very old house. There's cracks all in the walls and we get very cold in the winter. We don't have any electricity or indoor plumbing. You'll have to go down to the spring for water. That building out back is the outhouse. You'll find an old Sears & Roebuck catalog laying there. And you'll have to go up on the mountain to chop wood for the fireplace and cook stove.

"We go down to the creek to wash. And we are always on the look-out for the copperheads and rattlers .

"Rabbits are pretty easy to trap. Sometimes we get a squirrel or a bird. Every now and then we get a raccoon. Tasty eating. Young coons are best eating. Older ones are too fatty."

"Grandpa, I haven't had anybody to talk to since my daddy died."

"Son, remember, your daddy was my son, and I think he and I were a lot alike. Why, I imagine you're going to grow up to be just like me and just like him, too." Grandpa had a little smile on his face as he lit up his old pipe. The tobacco smelled like cherry.

Finally Grandma called us to dinner. I could hardly wait! From the way Grandpa gulped down his soup, he was as hungry as I was. Soon he said, "You through with that stew?" Danny nodded. "Crop'll be in a'fore long. We've got some radishes, onions and taters in the ground, some tomatoes about to bloom, and a small stand of corn. It's that time of year where we'll be fatter'n a hog.

"Well, let's go out on the front porch and let me tell you all about your daddy and your new home. Having you here is almost like having your daddy back home."

"Grandpa, why did my daddy have to die?" I felt those all too familiar tears stinging at my eyes.

"Son' your daddy was a soldier. And sometimes things go wrong. What you need to remember, though, is your daddy was a very brave man. He saved the lives of a lot of people. They wrote all about it in the Scottsboro Sentinel newspaper. The newspaper

over in Huntsville, The Huntsville Times, even wrote about it. Everybody here in Rattlesnake Cove knows what a brave man your daddy was. They all remember him from before he went off to the second war. He was so polite and respectful to everybody. He had nice manners, and he would always do everything he could to help people. Your daddy was a good man.

"And, Danny, did you know that I was in the first war? They sent me all over France and Germany. I'll tell you about France tomorrow. Maybe you'll go there some day. But right now, it's almost dark out and you need to get to bed. Your grandmother has a pallet fixed for you in the kitchen. Sorry our house is so small. We just have the kitchen and the bed room. You go get some sleep. We've got a lot of chores in the morning and I'll tell you a lot more. We have lots of time to talk.

Danny started toward the door, tired and ready for sleep, but turned back to Grandpa and blurted out the question that had been gnawing at him ever since he left Tennessee. "Just one more thing, Grandpa. Do you know where my brothers are?"

"Son, I wish I knew. All I know is they were there one day and gone the next. I have no idea. Something's bad wrong. Makes me so sad and I feel so helpless to do anything about it. It breaks my heart. I pray for them every time I sit down and talk with the Lord." Danny fought back the tears that were stinging his eyes. His throat felt tight. Grandma had walked out onto the porch in time to hear his question

"G-good night, Grandpa. Good night, Grandma." he managed.

"Good night, Danny," they both gave him a good hug.

The last glow of the sun slowly faded behind the mountains in the west, as the moon rose, shining brightly though the trees.

"It's a full moon night. Almost like daylight," thought Danny.

I feel so happy. First time I've been so peaceful since before my daddy went off to war. Danny started wondering about why he was being treated so good by people he didn't even know. "Is this for real?" he asked himself.

"Grandpa, why are you waking me up so early?" The boy muttered as he tried to open his eyes.

"You're living in the country now, Danny. The sun is almost up already. And that's why those roosters are crowing. They're telling you to get up. We've got a mule to feed, a cow to milk, and a hog to slop. And somebody's got to build Grandma a fire in the cook stove if we're going to have any breakfast. And, after all that, we've got to chop some wood!

"Tell you what, you take the pail down to the spring and get us some fresh water. I'll build the fire. Hope we have enough kindling from yesterday. After breakfast we'll go check on the potatoes and corn. Sure do hope they start putting out soon or I don't know what we're going to do for food."

"Yes, Sir, I'm on my way down to the spring," as Danny grabbed the pail.

"You watch out for snakes, now. Remember what I told you."

The spring flowed out of the rocks on the side of a hill, fresh and clear. Moss grew on the rocks and all around it. It got slippery right up next to the water. But Danny got the water without mishap.

The boy felt so happy that he could do something to help his grandparents. He sat down on a small boulder, after checking carefully for snakes, and pulled his harmonica out of the fishing bag that he always carried. 'Danny Boy' seemed the right song to play. "Daddy told me the song is about a young man who travels far away and his grandfather is sad because he thinks his grandson, Danny, will never return," Danny thought. "I've never been to Rattlesnake Cove before but I feel like I have come home. I am home!"

His arm started aching with the weight of the heavy pail of water, as he struggled up the hill from the spring. He stopped several times and put the pail down, rubbing his hand where the handle was starting to cut in. "This kind of work will take some getting used to, he thought."

Grandma already had breakfast on the table when Danny came in. It all smelled so good. Grandpa opened the door for him and hoisted the heavy water pail up on the wash table. "I heard you playing my favorite song," Grandpa smiled. "Sounded mighty good."

We sat around the table in the kitchen and Grandpa asked the Lord to bless our food. It was wonderful. Eggs, corn bread, just a small piece of bacon, and coffee. The cow wasn't giving milk lately, they said.

"I love you, Danny," Grandma stated. "Hope you enjoy your breakfast. It's not much but it's all we have."

"Breakfast was so good, Grandma. Thank you!"

"Do you think after we get through eating you can go pick us some poke salad? It's growing out front. I'll show you where. Tonight I'll mix it up with some eggs and a little bacon grease for supper. It'll be good with corn bread."

"That's a fine idea, Lu, Grandpa replied. The big man turned to his grandson, "Danny, why don't I show you how to dig up sassafras root? We'll have sassafras tea with our supper."

"Y'all are so good to me! I'll be fat as a pig if you keep feeding me like this. I'll be glad to dig it up. Why don't I get us some rabbit for supper too? I bet I can scare up some. I learned how while we were living in the desert. In fact, I bet I can get us squirrels too, if you want some." Danny thought of all the years he had gone hungry, rarely having a meal at all.

As the days went by, Danny learned about his new home. He learned his chores, that he happily did. "Such a good place to live. These people really do seem to love me," Danny thought. "And I, for sure, love them!"

"Danny, here, take these scraps out and throw them to the chickens. We don't waste nothing around here. When you get through look around and see if you can find some eggs. The peddler will be around after a while and I need some corn meal and some flour." Grandma instructed.

"Ma'am? Grandma, what's eggs have to do with corn meal and flour?"

"We trade, Grandson, we trade. We ain't got no money. Everybody trades. It's all we can do. Praise the Lord for the Social Security check we get first of the month. Go look up under the house and around the shed. That's where chickens like to lay." Her chickens wandered, at will, clucking and scratching all over the yard and across the road.

"After you get through gathering the eggs, Grandpa wants to take you to chop some wood. Hurry up, He's calling you now."

"Be right there, Grandpa," Danny shouted. "Grandma wants

me to look for chicken eggs first before the peddler gets here."

'Let's see now, under the house, and around the shed. There, I see a whole mess of eggs." Danny gathered them quickly, putting them in the basket she had handed him.

"Grandma, I found nine eggs. Think that's enough?"

"I hope it is, Danny. I'll just have to talk to the peddler and pray. He's a God-fearing man. It'll be all right. Thank you. Go on now and help Grandpa."

'"Danny, how many eggs did you find?"

"Nine, Grandpa. Grandma was afraid it might not be enough."

"We'll get by, Danny. We always do. Now let me show you how to hold this ax. Place your hand right up next to the blade. Careful now, I keep it very sharp. You see, if you carry it by the end of the handle you're liable to swing it and do something bad. Also, when you do swing it to cut wood, you place your right hand up towards the blade. And your left hand towards the end of it. Then you put all your strength into your right hand as you bring the blade against the wood. You are right handed?" Danny nodded yes.

"Whatever you do you always look all around you when you are handling the ax and you always hold it tight in your hands so it doesn't swing out. You can really hurt somebody with this. Here's a nice little tree to start off with. I'll cut it down and you watch. Stand back now. There you go. Notch it on one side and then take it down from the other side. OK, your turn. Here, try this little tree. Danny did as he was instructed, and the small tree fell just right.

"Now, that I've shown you how to cut down trees, Danny, let me show you the smart way. You see, these woods are thousands of years old, and there's trees everywhere that have already fallen down and dried out. That's what we want to take home. You may already know that the dried wood is what we want to burn. Tell you what, let's just drag those two home, the ones over there. Careful of that ax, now. Don't stumble. We'll get them home and then we'll cut them up for firewood so they'll fit in the stove and in the fireplace. Uh Oh, I hear Grandma calling."

"Y'all finish up all your chores. Grandpa will show you what to do. Then come on here in the kitchen with me. I want to tell you about church tomorrow."

"Yes, Grandma." They both said at the same time.

Anxious to get back to find out what Grandma had to tell them, Danny listened carefully and followed the instructions Grandpa gave him. They worked hard cutting, hauling and chopping the wood as well as the usual farm chores. Danny was finding out how much it took to keep Grandma's cook stove going and for the fireplaces.

"Here I am, Grandma. I slopped the hog, milked the cow, and gathered your eggs. I even chopped wood. Tomorrow, after church, Grandpa says he's going to take me fishing."

"Thank you for gathering up those eggs, Danny. They were just enough for me to get a little meal and flour from the peddler. Grandson, you are such a fine young man. Just like your daddy before he went off to war the first time. But you ain't got no clothes. You've worn what you've got on since you got here. I looked in an old trunk and found some of your daddy's things. You're almost the same size he was. Here, try on this shirt and pants. Why, I even found his shoes. He said he'd be wearing army boots and wouldn't need his shoes.

"Go wash up good, then take them in the other room and try them on." Danny was glad to get washed up and he was anxious to put on the same clothes his daddy had worn.

"Lu Ann," Grandpa said to Grandma, "you be sure to introduce him to Maggie Ann tomorrow at church. We need for him to grow up and stay right here in Rattlesnake Cove. We can't have him going off to Tennessee and marrying some woman up there like his daddy did."

"Daniel, you hush, he'll hear us talking about him."

"I don't care. He's a fine young man and I make no secret about wanting him to stay here the rest of his life."

"Daniel, our grandson is going to grow up to be a big important man some day. All we can do is guide him and teach him how a man should live. Then we need to pray that we are around long enough to see what he becomes. Meanwhile, let's take him to church tomorrow and help him learn about the Lord."

"Grandma, Grandpa," as he burst into the room, "these clothes fit perfect. Thank you so much. Can we go outside on the porch and watch the sun go down? It is so peaceful and quiet here. I love it here. I love y'all."

"Well, for a few minutes," said Grandpa, "after the sun goes down it'll be so dark you can't see nothing. Clouds are comin' in and may block the moon. Won't be like that full moon last night. It gets dark in these hills. After you lay down to sleep you need to listen very carefully. The hills come alive with owls, raccoons, bobcats, and other critters. They'll sing you to sleep. Get a good night's sleep and after breakfast in the morning I'll show you how to hitch up the mule to our wagon, for us to go to church.

Chapter 5

The Lord's Day in Rattlesnake Cove, Alabama

Grandma, is the preacher going to talk all day?" Whispered Danny.

"You just hush and be still."

"Grandma, who is that girl over there? She's cute as a button."

"Shhhhh!"

"Let's all stand for our closing song," said the preacher in his booming deep voice.

"Finally," Danny thought, after they all sang about gathering at the river.

Grandma says, "Come with me, son, I want you to meet somebody."

"Hello, Danny," said the cutest girl

on this side of the world. Danny got so tongue tied he couldn't speak.

"You know me?" he blurted out.

"Sure, I'm Maggie Ann. Everybody in Rattlesnake Cove knows who you are. They say your daddy was a hero. They say President Eisenhower himself gave your daddy a medal for saving people's lives. I saved all the newspaper clippings. I'll show them to you some day.

"My daddy went fishing with your daddy. Our daddy's even went over to Huntsville and played music on Saturday nights. The Snuff Dippers Ball, they called it. Mama said it was a honkytonk. My daddy played left handed guitar and your daddy played the harmonica. Made some good money, too, my daddy said"

"But isn't your daddy the preacher?"

"Yes, folks around here ain't got no money to pay Daddy, so somebody always invites us over to eat after church. But Daddy still goes over to Huntsville to play on Saturday nights. It's all the cash we got."

Danny stammered "Our dads were friends? Ain't that something! Say, my Grandpa and I are going fishing after church. Wanna come along? You can tell me more about our dads."

"I can't," Maggie Ann said. We're invited to eat at somebody's house. Chicken as usual, I'm sure."

"What about tomorrow afternoon? Meet you at the oak trees?"

Maggie Ann replied "I'll slip out some food from the table today and bring it for our lunch. But a lot of times there's not much left for us kids after the grown-ups get through eating. If my daddy doesn't stop eating so much chicken he's gonna start clucking like one. Anyway, See ya tomorrow with whatever I can slip out."

"I'll try to finish up my chores early. I always have hooks and line in my fishing bag. See ya tomorrow. Bye."

It was a long afternoon and night until the next morning and a rush, rush, rush with all the chores.

"Hey, Maggie Ann. Glad you made it. I dug up some worms for us. Can I bait your hook for you?"

"Sure, Danny, but why don't we eat first, before we get our hands dirty? Danny looked at his grubby hands. I brought us a couple of chicken legs, some corn bread, and a jug of tea."

"Great, I'm starving. Been working hard all morning trying to get my chores done. Let's sit on this rock over here, but first I need to wash up in the river."

"Careful" Maggie Ann yelled. "You've got to look all around the rocks all the time. They just ain't safe. They named this place Rattlesnake Cove for a reason. They usually leave you alone unless you scare them. They're not all that bad. They're good eating if you know how to cook them. Anyhow, let's get to eating right now. Here, you take the biggest chicken leg. You're a big man."

"Well, I'm not exactly a man yet, but thank you. Tell me, what do you know about my daddy? I want to learn all I can about him."

"Danny, all I really know is what my daddy said about your daddy. He says your daddy was just about the best man he ever knew. Your daddy was right with God and always knew the right thing to do when there were problems. He says whenever anybody needed help your daddy was right there. He says your daddy felt he needed to go to war because that was that's what Americans do. Your daddy and my daddy signed up for World War Two together."

"I want to grow up just like my daddy. Did your daddy go to France and Germany too, like mine? Daddy told me so many stories about over there."

Maggie Ann smiled and replied "Oui, oui."

Danny questioned "Huh?"

"That's what daddy always says when I ask him for something. Took me a long time before I realized he was teasing me. Daddy

finally told me they spell the words O-U-I and that it means 'yes'. Sounds kinda funny to me. But it doesn't matter. I want to go there some day, especially to Paris. I want folks to treat me so polite and say 'Oui, madam'."

SPLASH!

"Maggie Ann, did you see that? Them fish, they's a'jumpin'. Let's get our lines in. Fish for supper tonight!

A short while later Maggie Ann yelled, "Danny, you got it! Oh wait, there's my line now. Got it!" She giggled as she hauled the wriggling fish in.

"Maggie Ann, we're gonna have a mess of fish to take home. I love fishing with you. You're good luck."

"Danny, ain't no luck to it. You know what you're doing. Say, what all do you have in that bag of yours? You carry it every-where."

"Well, lots of things. I've got my daddy's harmonica, for one.

My daddy said he took it all over France and Germany. He said when the evenings got peaceful and quiet he would play it. He taught me to play it too. Wanna hear?"

"Can you play I'll Fly Away?"

"Of course, here goes."

Sweet plaintive notes floated from the harmonica as Maggie Ann began to sing along.

Hey, that was pretty. You sure can carry a tune, Maggie Ann. I can play 'Danny Boy.' Do you know the words?"

"Yep, I sure do. That's a good Irish song. My daddy plays it for me on his guitar."

As Danny played the first few notes Maggie Ann joined in with her clear angelic voice.

"Danny, the sun's getting low in the sky. I guess we need to get on home. But first, I want to ask you something."

"OK, what's on your mind?"

"Danny, my daddy tells me you're going to be a big important man some day and travel all over the world. He says you're going to do big things just like your daddy did. Will you re-member me?"

"I can't imagine what makes your daddy think that. Rattlesnake Cove is my home and I ain't going nowhere. Now, let's get on home. Can we go fishing again sometime?"

Two nice trout for each of them. As they gathered up their lines and fish Danny's hand accidentally touched Maggie Ann's.

"Oh, I'm so sorry," the very embarrassed Danny stuttered.

Maggie Ann just smiled. She already knew Danny was going to be her man some day.

"Bye, Maggie Ann."

"See ya, Danny."

Danny whistled and skipped all the way home.

"Grandma, look what I've got us? A mess of trout. We're gonna eat good tonight."

"Grandson, you are so good for us. You help with all the chores and then you go get us fish. How would we get by without you?" Grandpa smiled. "Look who we got here."

"Hello, Danny, I'm your aunt Janie Sue. Your daddy was my brother. I sat and cried all night when we all heard what happened. And I worried about you. Your daddy took you off and I never got to see you after you were born. But we kept up with you. Here, stand up in front of me and let me look at you. You're such a handsome young man. Just like your daddy. She put her hands on his shoulders.

"I come to visit my parents, your grandparents, all the time because I worry about them so much. Your grandmother has spells and your Grandpa can't walk good. I'm so glad you're here to help them. Here, let me hug you."

"I'm so happy to see you, Aunt Janie Sue. Daddy told me all about you. I think he missed you a lot. Can I come visit you some time?"

"Of course, Danny, you're my blood kin. You are always welcome at my house. I only live right down the road. Come over any time. I'll cook you up some corn bread and a mess of potatoes."

Danny slept good that night. A good fish dinner and he got to meet his daddy's sister.

"Good morning, Grandma. Good morning, Grandpa. I got up before the roosters crowed me up this morning. Today is going to be such a beautiful day."

Chapter 6

Rattlesnake Church Service

D anny, you hurry up with all your chores. We're going somewhere special this afternoon," Grandpa said.

"Where, Grandpa? Tell me about it, please?"

"There's gonna be a snake service today over at Grandpa Pickett's home. There's this man from over about Sand Mountain somewhere who claims the Bible says that if you're a man of God snakes can't hurt you. Well, I have my own feelings about that. We go outta curiousness but mostly cause we get to see our friends and neighbors. It'll be something new for you to see. Go on, now, and get us some firewood chopped up."

"Grandpa, I think all that stuff's silly. I bet he just comes here to find more rattlesnakes."

"Danny, you may think it's silly. I do too. But don't ever make fun of a man's religion. Just respect it and go on about your way. Go on now, that woods a'waitin'."

Later that day after plenty of firewood was cut, hogs slopped,

chickens fed, and water brought up from the spring, Danny got cleaned up and ran into the house. "Grandpa! Grandma! I got the mules and wagon all hitched up. Y'all about ready?"

"Hold on, grandson. Women just seem to take a little.longer. You'll understand some day."

Danny sat at the table with Grandpa, fidgeting as they waited for Grandma to put the final touch on her hair and clothes. The excitement was building to see how these people worship with snakes. He meant no disrespect, as Grandpa had told him, but it was a very different church service to what he had seen in the past.

"LuAnn, you look mighty fine," Grandpa said to Grandma. "You're worth the wait." Grandpa helped Grandma down the porch steps then said, "All right, Grandson, help your grandmother up into the wagon and let's go."

"Grandpa, you're taking us down a road I haven't seen before." They were traveling a road that cut deep into the woods.

"Danny, see that hillside up there? That's where your daddy shot a young buck. Kept us fed almost all winter. We're almost there. Now you watch yourself when we get there. Stay away from the preacher. No telling what that preacher is gonna do; might hand you one of his pets." The old man chuckled.

"Grandpa, I can hear them from here. I never heard so much noise in all my borned days. The shouting and carrying on. That must be a bunch of crazy people in there. And that's about God?"

"Grandson, they believe it is. Let's go in now and keep an eye out around you."

"Grandpa, that man has a whole bunch of snakes wrapped around his hand. And they're rattlesnakes. Look at that triangle head and look at those markings. They'll kill you.

"Grandpa, those people are all jumping up and down and they're singing so loud and clapping their hands and banging on stuff. And that snake preacher is spinning around and around with snakes all over him. He's as windy as a sackful of farts."

"Danny Carmichael! You mind your mouth. That kind of talk ain't gentleman like!" Grandma said crossly.

Danny muttered that he was sorry. He sat quietly when, suddenly he saw a "big'un" slither down the preacher's back and quickly out a hole in the floor.

"Grandpa, I've gotta go to the outhouse."

"Hush, Danny, you went just before we got here." Grandma said.

"Gotta go, Grandma," as he grabbed his fishing bag and ran for the door.

"I'm gonna catch that rattler," Danny said to himself. He pulled his daddy's knife out of the bag and cut a forked stick off

a tree. Shaking the stick under the house, in the bushes and around the big rocks. Finally there it was. Danny forked it and quickly cut off the head.

After burying

the head, just to be sure, Danny looked about for something to wrap the rest of it in. "There, on the clothesline is a towel," he thought. "Perfect." Danny wrapped the still writhing snake in the towel and hid it in the back of the wagon, then casually walked back into the service. "Weird how the muscles still seem to work even after the head is chopped off." he thought. He entered just as the last few rhythmic notes are played and the clapping stopped.

"You missed the whole service, Danny. Why are you smiling so much? You look as happy as a dead pig in the sunshine," whispered Grandpa. Danny gave him a wink, then took Grandma's arm.

"Come on, Grandma, I'll help you into the wagon, I've got a surprise for you when we get home." said Danny as he slyly looked in the back and saw the towel- wrapped, dead snake wriggling about.

Danny whistled all the way home.

"I'll unhitch the mule and put up the wagon, Grandpa." Jumping down quickly to help Grandma. He didn't want anyone to see the snake and spoil his surprise.

A few minutes later, after skinning the snake and pulling out the innards, Danny walked in the house and announced "Look what we have for supper!"

"Land sakes alive! What are you doing with that thing? Get it outta here!"

"But Grandma, this is supper. I'll grill it outside myself if you want me to. I caught them all the time in the desert. They're not bad eating. I wonder what that snake preacher will think when he sees he's missing one," laughed Danny.

Grandma replied, "Danny, I've got a mind to tan your hide for scaring me so bad. But, you take it on outside and grill it. Food is food. I'll whip up some fried potatoes and onions to go with it. Yes, I know you sneaked that over on me; going to the out-house my foot! You're grinning like a possum eatin' a sweet tater."

After dinner they all sat out on the porch enjoying the cool mountain breeze and listening to the symphony of cicadas and wild night animals with an occasional owl and sometime even a bobcat cry.

Danny started back to school. He and Maggie Ann had classes together. They learned English, math, geography, history, and even a little music and art. The years went by. Birthdays went by.

Christmas time meant a few simple presents, singing, laughter, and a music special at church. Danny began to eat a lot of chicken at Maggie Ann's home, so much that he, too, felt like he might start clucking, just like Maggie Ann's daddy. Her brother got caught by the law once and lost his car, But he found another immediately. Danny wondered about it, but knew not to ask too many questions. Danny and Maggie Ann slipped away from the others whenever they could to walk, holding hands, and steal a kiss or two. Nobody asked about it. The preacher was happy for his daughter and Danny's grandparents were also happy.

Maggie Ann was now the church pianist. Her left-handed guitar playing, preacher daddy realized that notes on a piano were the same as on a guitar. Then it was just a matter of figuring out which notes for which chords. Together they could play a foot stomping "Come to Jesus." Danny's favorite song was the Hank Williams favorite, "I Saw The Light."

Whenever they could get a ride and had the money they went to the movies at the theater in Fort Payne. "Ben-Hur," starring Charlton Heston, had just finished playing. They saw "Some Like It Hot" starring Marilyn Monroe and Tony Curtis. All the young ladies started dressing like Marilyn and bleaching their hair blonde like Marilyn. Marilyn Monroe was the most beautiful woman in the world, or so Danny thought.

All the church people were aghast at the new singing star, Elvis Presley. Those vulgar movements he made two years ago on the Ed Sullivan Show were more than most country people could handle. Maggie Ann and Danny listened to him on the radio whenever her preacher daddy was not around. Maggie Ann memorized every word to "Love Me Tender", "Don't Be Cruel" and "Teddy Bear."

General Eisenhower was still president. The 48 United States became 50 United States with both Alaska and Hawaii being added.

The world was in good shape.

After four years living in Rattle Snake Cove Danny now knew he was at home.

One fateful morning, April 1959

"Good morning, Rooster, I hear you. Fooled you. I was already awake," Danny stretched and said out loud, to himself, "Up, up, up! I've gotta get up and do my chores." He thought, "Maybe I can get through in time to go fishing with Maggie Ann."

"Danny, your grandma's already got plenty of kindling and wood to cook breakfast. While she's doing that let's go up the mountain a little ways and chop some wood. We can stockpile some for later. It'll get us a good start on the day" The old man said.

"Sure, I'll get the ax."

"This is a mighty steep hill, Grandpa, lots of loose gravel. It's rained a lot lately and it's slippery too."

"Yes, you just watch your step, Grandson."

Suddenly,"Oh, oh, oh, help me! help me!" Grandpa yelled as he fell, then tumbled and rolled over and over down the hill over the sharp rocks. There was blood on the side of his head.

"Grandpa! Grandpa, Are you alright? You've hurt your head, what can I do?"

"I can't move, son,"he gasped. "I heard my leg snap so don't try to move me. Get your water jug and splash some on my face. You go down the hill and tell your grandma. Then you run down the road and get your aunt Janie Sue. She'll know what to do. I'm too big for you to pick up. I'll just lie here. I'll be all right. Tell her to hurry," whispered Grandpa in a very feeble voice.

It seemed like hours had gone by as Danny struggled to follow his grandfather's instructions. Grandma had sat down hard in her chair and begun to cry. He tried to comfort her but had to get to Janie Sue's fast.

Janie Sue quickly rounded up some neighbor men to help.

"Follow me, I'll show you where," Danny said to his aunt. "Grandpa's a big man. Sure am glad you found some men to

help. He had blood on the side of his head. I'm afraid he hit his head real hard. Heard a loud snap like a bone breaking, too."

Janie Sue dropped to her knees beside the still body of her father. "Daddy, Daddy, can you hear me?" pleaded Janie Sue. "It's no use," she finally said. "I can feel his heart and he's breathing, but he can't hear us. Danny, you run and get Preacher Wilburn. He's got some experience from when he was in the Army with your daddy."

When Danny and the Preacher arrived at the Carmichael home, he told Maggie Ann, who had insisted on coming, and Danny to stay with Grandma. He hurried up the hill to where the others had gathered.

"Maggie Ann, I'm so glad you came with your daddy. I'm really worried about Grandpa. I feel like it was my fault. I didn't watch him close enough. I knew it was wet and slippery. We was just starting up the mountain when he slipped."

"Danny, you can't blame yourself. I've helped Daddy a lot. He knows what he's doing. I'll stay with your Grandma. You go on up there, they will need you."

"Well, I've checked him all over and it looks like he's going to be OK. Best I can tell his spine is okay. His neck seems to be OK. Danny, you go down to the house and get a blanket. Make sure it's a good strong one. Tell Grandma what's going on. We're all going to have to pitch in and carry him down. We'll make a litter with the blanket and some poles." Preacher Wilburn finally answered everybody's unspoken questions and prayers. "I'll help you get him down, Then I'll get in my car and go to Bridgeport to get Doctor Mott."

"Grandma, Preacher Wilburn is already here and is taking care of him. I've got to get a strong blanket so they can carry him down. He can't walk. You just sit right here and I'll be right back." Danny ran to the old trunk where his father's things were kept. He found the strong wool blanket that Daddy had brought back from the second war.

Danny ran up the hill wondering where his strength was coming from. The preacher and others were waiting with poles they had cut. Soon they had Grandpa on the makeshift litter and down the hill. With much difficutly they got the old man into bed. The preacher ran to his car and headed to Bridgeport..

Hours later back at Grandpa's.

"Well, looks like all your prayers worked," Doctor Mott said. "He's going to live. Now that he's awake and is able to talk a little I can tell a lot more. He's going to be weak and laid up for some time. His right leg is broken. I think that splint I fixed up might hold it. I wish I had some medicine for him, but I do have some shine I keep for emergencies. Maybe that will help a little."

Maggie Ann pulled Danny aside and whispered "My brother, Roy, runs shine. He'll get you all you need."

"What do you mean 'runs shine', Maggie Ann?

"That's how my brother helps us make a living. The law claims you have to pay taxes on 'shine' but it don't make no sense. Taxes just makes everything cost more. Our country is founded on resisting taxes. Roy keeps his car hidden up on the mountain. With those heavy springs and that souped up engine he can carry a huge load and outrun any lawman around. He'll get your Grandpa all the pain killer he needs."

"You surprise me more every time I see you, Maggie Ann."

"You've got a long rough road ahead of you, Danny," Doctor Mott said. "Your Grandpa is bedridden and won't be able to get up for some time. You're going to have to turn him every hour or he'll get pneumonia. You're going to have to take care of their farm and your grandparents too. I checked your grandmother and she's not doing too well. She's already doing more than she is able to do."

"Doctor, I'll want to take care of my grandparents. They been taking care of me, now it's my turn to do for them." replied Danny.

"I'll be over after a while and bring something to eat. " Maggie Ann had been standing nearby while Danny talked with Dr. Mott. She squeezed her friend's arm and smiled at him.

"That'll be good, Maggie Ann. We can sit with the old folks and talk about the good old days. You can tell me more stories about your daddy and all that time he spent with mine."

"I'll do everything I can do to help. I'll be over all the time," offers Janie Sue. "We'll get through this."

That evening, as promised, Maggie Ann knocked on the screen door. "Daddy brought me over in his car. He said he'll be back after a while," Maggie Ann said. "I brought some corn bread Mama cooked and a mason jar of tea. Is your Grandpa up to company for a minute?"

Danny ushered her into the little room that served as kitchen and sitting space. "Gee, glad you got to come."

"He's still real groggy but you can go speak to him if you want. He mumbles a little but that's mostly about it. He's really worried about Grandma and so am I."

"Well, I want to see both of them for a minute, and then we can sit in the swing on the front porch. We can hear them if they need us." She Gave Grandma a big hug and fixed her a plate of cornbread and a glass of tea. The old lady picked at the food and only drank a few sips of the cool sweet tea. Maggie Ann helped her onto the bed to rest beside her husband. Grandpa hadn't awakened through it all. She joined Danny on the porch.

"It sure is nice here out here, Danny. I love the sound of the creaking swing and the "mountain orchestra." The tree frogs and crickets chirping, the hooting of the owls, the skittering sounds of the raccoons, and even the bobcat screeching. It's all given to us by God. This whole cove is like Heaven. I would never want to live anywhere else."

"I like the way you talk, Maggie Ann, and the beautiful words you make. I wish I could talk like that."

"You can, Danny. I learned from my daddy. He's a very smart man. Daddy told me that he and your daddy would lie awake at night in France when there was no shooting and listen to all the sounds in the woods. Says it was like music. Wouldn't it be wonderful to go to France and all those fancy places our daddy's went?

"After the Army Daddy went to school at Howard College down in Birmingham. It was all paid for by the GI bill. That's how he learned to be a preacher. Daddy is passionate about saving souls. Some day you could go to school, too."

"Yes, you're right. But right now I'm worried about what to do for my grandparents. It's going to be an awful lot of work. Say, talking with you makes me feel a lot better. Can I hold your hand while we talk?"

"Yes, Danny," as she timidly stuck out her hand. "It feels all tingly when you touch my hand. I could sit here all night listening to the mountain orchestra and looking up at the stars while we hold hands."

"I'm so glad I came to Rattlesnake Cove, I could never imagine living anywhere else. This is my home, Maggie Ann, I'm not going anywhere, ever. My heart is here in Rattlesnake Cove with you."

"Oh Danny, do you mean that?"

"You bet I do. Oh, here comes your daddy now. Can I give you a good night hug?"

"Yes, I'd like that. But make sure you go over and say good night to my daddy, also."

Next morning Janie Sue walked into the house and asked, "Danny, how's it going? We've all been so worried about my folks and you, too."

"Aunt Janie Sue, it's getting hard. I'm falling behind on everything. I just can't keep up with the animals, turn Grandpa, and help Grandma get around. And I don't know how to cook. And that's not even counting washing the clothes."

"Danny, we've been talking about you and trying to figure out how to help. The only thing I can figure out is to move my mama and daddy down to our house and have them live with us. Then I've got my husband and kids to help. We'll move their bed into the bedroom. Two of our kids are already sleeping on the floor. But we'll get by."

"But what about me?"

"Danny, your daddy and my husband never got along. You see,

my husband runs a moonshine still. He takes care of us real good and when the law picks him up they never keep him more than two or three days at a time. Truth be known the law is some of my husband's best customers. But your daddy said that was illegal. Your daddy never understood we were just trying to get by. So there was a lot of bad blood. My husband just won't allow you to stay with us.

"Danny, my property down the road is half of your grandparents property. When I got married they said they'd go ahead and give me my half. This half of the property will belong to you. Rattlesnake Cove will always be your home."

"But what about right now?"

His aunt hesitated, looking away. "Danny, I've kept in touch with your mama. They're living in Chicago now. She said she'd like you to come up there and live with them."

"And Buford?

"Yes, Danny, he's there. But your mama says Buford has changed. He's stopped drinking and he's got a job too."

Chapter 7

On the Way To Chicago

Danny, here's some money to buy you a bus ticket. You'll have to go to Chattanooga to catch it. I hope it's enough. Greyhound goes through here, but they won't stop to pick up folks. I'll see about getting you a ride to Chattanooga. Here's your mama's address in Chicago."

After Janie Sue hugged him and turned away Danny looked up at the porch ceiling and studied a cobweb while he fought the tears stinging is eyes. Then he slumped down in a chair, trying to make himself as small as possible; he wanted to disappear. "It's happening again," He thought. "It's been a wonderful four years here. I thought I was home for good but Rattlesnake Cove was just another stop in a rough road."

Janie Sue and some neighbors had come at the rooster's crow that morning and packed up Grandpa's and Grandma's things and moved them to her house. Grandpa looked so sad, although he said nothing. Danny could hear Grandma's soft sobs. He tried to comfort her as best he could, but she was leaving her home and Danny feared it would kill her. Saying good-bye to them nearly killed him.

About mid-morning Danny heard the sound of a car and recognized it as the preacher's rattley old ride. Maggie Ann jumped out of the car and ran to Danny.

"Oh Danny, I don't want you to go. I'll miss you," she wept. "I always knew you would have leave some day. I'm so scared you will go away and forget about me."

"This is my home. Wherever I go I'll always come back. My heart is here in Rattlesnake Cove with you. My heart will always be with you. I mean it. I promise I'll never forget you."

"I just know you will be a big important man some day. You will travel around the world and meet lots of people and do many things. I just hope that you won't forget me and you'll come back here some day."

"I'm so glad my daddy offered to take you to Chattanooga. This way I can spend time with you on the way and stay with you until you get on the bus."

Danny finally remembered his manners, and tried to sound cheerful. "Morning, Preacher Wilburn. I guess Janie Sue must've ask you to take me to Chattanooga. Mighty nice of you."

"Hop in the car, you two, we need to get on down the road. I think there's a 5 P.M. bus from Chattanooga." Preacher Wilburn looked back at Danny, "Son, when I was going to school at Howard College down in Birmingham they told me that whenever I give a speech or a talk I should condense it to three main points. Any less you're not saying much; any more, and the message gets all confusing. So I'd like to make my three main points to you. Number one: Always treat people right. Number two: Learn from everybody, wherever you go. And number three is very important, get yourself an education."

Sir, what you say makes good sense. I'll try to do all you say. You and Mrs. Wilburn have been like family to me and I have come to respect you very much. Thank you. And thank you and Maggie Ann for taking me to Chattanooga."

Danny sadly looked at their fishing spot as they passed. Then their oak tree. There was the church. Would he ever see all this again? Would he ever see Maggie Ann again? He knew he promised but still the thought of life somewhere else without her and without his grandparents scared him. He thought he had a home, but once again he was wrong.

Maggie Ann placed her hand on Danny's nervous quivering hand. She asked Danny to tell about capturing a rattlesnake at the snake service. Preacher Wilburn laughed and laughed. That was the funniest thing he had ever heard. This young man fit into their life so well. He was perfect for Maggie Ann. But right now they needed to do some growing up, he thought.

The bus station in Chattanooga was the busiest place Danny had ever seen. People milling around everywhere. Carrying suitcases or duffle bags. Fathers with bus schedules in their hands and mothers with small children in tow holding tightly to their hands to prevent them from running off and being lost in the ever moving crowd. Danny suddenly felt very small and alone. He turned and reached for the only form of belonging that he could find and found Maggie Ann's petite hand. It was soft and warm and he thought for a minute that he might never be able to let go, for if he did he feared he would never know this kind of connection with anyone ever again. His thoughts were interrupted by her father gently clearing his throat, "Time's getting close now, Danny. Here, I've got a little money for you. I think you'll need it. I'll give you and Maggie Ann a few minutes by yourself while I go get us a couple of sandwiches and a cup of coffee. Danny and Maggie Ann went to the ticket window. "A one way ticket to Chicago, Illinois, please."

"Let's just sit here and hold hands a few minutes, Danny." Danny took the opportunity to lean over and give her a soft kiss and a big hug, before her daddy returned. Again, Danny wondered if he would ever feel this way in the days and years ahead. Was it even possible? Probably not, given where he was going and the life that most certainly awaited him in Chicago.

"Here's the bus now," Preacher Wilburn announced as he walked up. Better say bye real quick. He handed Danny a sandwich wrapped in plain white paper. The boy shook hands with the man who had befriended him and helped him in countless ways. "Good Bye, Sir. I can never thank you enough." After thanking the preacher Danny shoved the sandwich into his coat pocket and then turned to Maggie Ann.

"Danny, I want to add one more thing," smiled Maggie Ann. Never forget me. You are my very best friend."

"Bye, Maggie Ann. I'll be back." Danny squeezed her hand.

"You better," she winked.

Danny boarded the big Greyhound bus and waved out the window as the bus engines roared and it started moving.

Knoxville, Lexington, Indianapolis. 23 hours on the road. Once again, everybody offering him a drink from their brown paper bag. Others offered him funny smelling cigarettes. Once again he spent his birthday on the road. This time between Knoxville and Cincinnati. Danny was now 16.

Finally Chicago. The biggest buildings Danny had ever seen. Thousands and thousands of people. Everybody moving fast everywhere. People dressed in strange clothes and speaking languages he couldn't understand. Danny wondered if he was still in America.

Chapter 8

Shining Shoes In Chicago, Illinois

C*hicago: Pizzas, hot dogs, gourmet meals, jazz, Al Capone, Lake Michigan beach, and Lincoln Park.*

Chicago has it all. It is whatever you make it.

Named chicagoua after the garlic plant by early settlers Chicago rapidly grew because of what was a short stretch of about eight miles, known as the Chicago Portage. The Chicago Portage enabled travelers to take a short canoe trip between the great lakes and the Mississippi River, Thus allowing the entire world, all of Europe and other points, to travel through the Great Lakes all the way to New Orleans. In 1848 the first rail lines were constructed leading to Chicago becoming the beef market of America. Cattle from across the nation were shipped by rail to the Chicago Stockyards.

In 1871 the Chicago Tribune reported the great Chicago fire was started by Catherine O'Leary's cow. Even though later proven false the legend remains because the fire did start in her barn. 300 people died, 18,000 buildings were destroyed and nearly 100,000 of the city's 300,000 residents were left homeless.

Chicago quickly grew to be a gambling and gangster town because of natives like Al Capone. On Valentine's Day, 1929, seven people were shot down by people dressed as Chicago policemen at 2122 North Clark Street, in the near north Lincoln Park area. Many people believed Al Capone's gang members did the shooting, but it was never proven.

Lincoln Park, on the near north side of Chicago, is well known for its zoo, its lake and the relaxing trees that make it a popular relaxation spot for Chicago natives.

Chicago has over a dozen sandy beaches along Lake Michigan for sun bathing and swimming.

Chicago's museums are the bright spots. The Art Institute of Chicago, on Michigan Avenue, founded in 1879, has over 300,000 works of art by artists such as van Gogh, Cezanne, and Picasso. A great place to learn art's contribution to mankind.

The incredible Museum of Science and Industry, bordering on Lake Michigan, has trains, planes, submarines, and coal mines. Their docents are very helpful in explaining the value of learning science.

The huge train systems in Chicago helped create the large international shipping port with ships from around the world.

After all the wars in Europe and the U.S. refugees began flooding into Chicago. Poles, Hungarians, Greeks, they all came.

Unfortunately the gangster history of Chicago, its "political machine" and the large mass of immigrants became a Mecca for miscreants who were very anxious to help the new immigrants part with their money.

A fter searching all over the bus station, Danny finally saw a sign that said "Information."

"Can you please help me, ma'am?"

"Here, son, you come over here and tell me where you want to go."

"Ma'am, I'm trying to go to this address and I have almost no money."

"Let's see now, you are going to 800 North State Street. That's almost downtown. Do you have any luggage?"

"No, ma'am, just my daddy's fishing bag."

"OK, best thing you can do is take the bus right over there," as she pointed outside, "to Michigan Avenue. Then get off and walk a couple streets over and you are right there. Since you've only got the one bag you'll be able to walk it OK. But watch out for pick pockets - people trying to rob you. And close the top of your bag. People will steal you blind. The bus will only cost you a dime. Any questions?"

"No, ma'am, thank you very much."

Danny stepped up on the bus and gave the driver a dime.

"I'm going to Michigan Avenue, can you please tell me when to get off?"

"Sure thing, Son," says the driver. "New to Chicago?"

"Yes sir."

"Well, here tell you what. Here's a booklet that will tell you how to get around this city. Chicago has the one of the best bus transit systems in the whole United States! You can go anywhere for just one thin dime," replied the kindly driver.

Danny observed the big city. People in a hurry to get somewhere. So many people. Lights everywhere. Cars, trucks, buses, bicycles. Just all a lot of confusion. But he stayed alert for Michigan Avenue.

"Time to get off, young man." Danny heard the driver shout over the noise. He started walking the direction the driver pointed. Finally, 800 North State Street. A tall, dingy apartment building with a shoe shop and cafe on the ground floor. Aunt Janie Sue's instructions said apartment 402 on the fourth floor.

Buford answered Danny's knock on the door. "We been expecting you, Boy. I'll tell you right now the way it is. I work like a dog to give your mama a place to live and I'm sure not going to support her brat. You can sleep here, but I'm not going to feed you. There's a blanket on the floor there. We got two rooms. A bedroom and a kitchen. Bathroom's down the hall. You can sleep on the floor in the kitchen."

"Yep, same 'ol Buford," Danny said to himself. The smell of whiskey was as strong as ever. Danny felt sick to his stomach.

"Where's my mama?"

"Don't you worry none about her. She'll be here when she gets here. And don't you be asking me any questions about anything. I don't want to see hide nor hair of you. Here's a key. You come and go whenever you want. But don't you ever knock on the door again because I'm not going to get up and answer it. You understand me?"

Danny stuck out his hand for the key and walked out the door. "When I need a place to sleep I'll come here, but not until," Danny mumbled to himself.

He ran down the stairs, two at a time, and when he reached the last one, he was standing in front of the shoe shop on the ground floor.

"Hello, can you help me, please?" Danny asked an elderly very respectable looking gentleman as he walked through the door.

"What do you need, young man?" replied the gentleman in a strong foreign accent.

"Sir, I just got here on a bus from Alabama. I haven't eaten in two days. My mama lives upstairs, but the man that lives with her won't let me eat. Says he doesn't want me around."

"You're talking about Buford, aren't you? " Asked the soft spoken older man. Danny nodded the affirmative. "Yes, we know that man. He keeps coal in the furnace for this building. Instead of paying him they let him use a small attic room. I think a woman stays with him."

"Sir, that woman is my mother. That's why I got sent here. I don't have anywhere else to go. I don't have any money. I just

don't know what to do."

"Well, I do run a shoe repair shop. Can you shine shoes?"

"Can I shine shoes!" answered Danny, brightening up at the prospect of a job. "Yes sir, and I can do the best spit shine you ever seen. My daddy was in the Army and he taught me how."

"You seem like a good kid. What's your name?"

"Danny. Danny Carmichael, Sir."

"Why don't you go on in the back and my wife, Karan, will fix you something to eat. Hope you like Greek food. My name is Cosmos." Cosmos called back to his wife, "We have a guest for lunch."

"I'm so hungry I could eat a bear."

"No bears around here, you'll have to settle for a souvlaki and perhaps Karan still has some honey topped pita toast for dessert!" Cosmos laughs. "After you eat we can talk more."

"Welcome. Come on back here," called a slight accented female voice, as Danny entered through a curtain on the door.

A pleasant looking lady with dark hair streaked with gray stood

at the stove, stirring something that smelled wonderful. She filled little bread pockets with the meat mixture she was stirring and served the starving boy.

"This is delicious, Ma'am, What do you call it?"

Karan replied in a heavy accent like her husband's, "That is souvlaki. It's meat wrapped in pita bread, with tomato and onion. You might call it a Greek hot dog."

"Tell me about yourself, Danny. What's in the bag you carry?" Cosmos asked.

"Well, my father made this bag for fishing and told me to keep it for him for when he returned from the war. We went fishing every chance we got. I have his flag, his medal for saving lives, some fishing hooks, flint stones, my father's harmonica, and my daddy's knife. My father was in World War Two and then again in Korea. But he didn't come back from Korea. Instead they had what they called a memorial service."

With every bite Danny told more of the story of how he had gotten to this point in his young but tumultuous life. He began with how he had run off the day of the memorial service and the trip with Mama and Buford. He fought to keep the tears at bay as he told them about his time in Alabama with his grandparents and the friends he had to leave behind there. He ended with seeing Buford in the apartment above the shoe shop.

"Buford hates me. Now he tells me I can sleep upstairs but he won't feed me. So that's how I ended up in front of your shop today. "

"Son, my wife and I escaped from Greece just after World War Two. It's because of soldiers like your father that we are able to be here in the greatest nation on earth. We love America. Let me tell you about our escape.

"First the Italians tried to invade us in 1940. After our brave Greek soldiers drove them back, the Germans came. The Germans destroyed our country: Our railroads, our ships, even our livestock. Our villages were burned. They burned our home, too. Our country had nothing. Then after that war we started fighting among ourselves in what they called a civil war. I didn't understand why we were fighting each other. We had nothing to fight about. Some people said it was over what type of government we should have. Democracy or Communist. Many countries sent us food and money but it was like a bribe; they mostly just wanted to take over. America sent a lot of food and money to help our country rebuild. But the communists had other ideas. When the civil war continued that's when we knew we had to leave our beloved Greece. It was no longer a country to live in. And we had very little money.

"Then we got an idea. Most of the ships had been destroyed but there were still a few. We started hanging around the docks. That's when we saw they often stacked up canvas on the decks. After learning that, we just had to watch for the right ship. Our Gypsy friends told us to watch for the flag the ships were flying. The French flag is blue, white, and red vertical stripes and that would be a good ship to get on. They also told us that when we walk up the plank to get on deck that we should act like we knew what we were doing, not like a tourist looking around a lot. Many people back then had forged papers, so they were on the look-out for people who seemed out of place. We were told to carry a few bundles of something and make it somewhat conceal our faces.

Finally we saw a ship that was flying the French flag. It was headed for Marseille, France, somebody said. We gathered up food and canteens of water and placed them in big boxes to help hide our faces. We waited until a bunch of people were walking  aboard, then we just walked along with everybody else and acted like we were working. We found canvas to hide under for three days until we made port in France. Our Gypsy friends in Greece had contacted their French counterparts who took us in until the right ship, heading for America, came along. We stowed away again. It was easy with so many people on board. After many days we saw the Statue of Liberty. That's when we walked off the ship to our new country.

"We had nothing except our desire to make a decent life together. After that, we made our way to Chicago and here we are today. Thousands and thousands of people from all over the world were flooding into the United States so it was easy to get past immigration people. We still have very little, just a shop and one small room where we sleep and eat. But we are together. We want to be American just like you. So we are taking citizenship classes."

Chapter 9

Danny Learns To Speak Greek

Cosmos paused and looked at Danny. "Why don't you tell me what you know about how to spit-shine shoes? I think we can work something out."

"Sir, my father always told me that when I grow up and look for a job or when I date a girl, that my shoes have to look the absolute best. He said anybody can get a haircut or put on fancy clothes and then develop a muscle man handshake, but it takes time and caring to make your shoes look good. He said that a man meeting his daughter's boyfriend for the first time, looks first at the shoes, then at his face. The father would feel that if the boy doesn't even take care of his shoes he is certainly not going to take care of his daughter. I want to be the very best man I can be in life, just like my father was. That's why I learned to shine shoes."

Danny hurried on, "My father said shining shoes is just good sense. They last longer when they are cared for. First you clean off all the dirt and grit, getting in the cracks real good. Use a little water if you have to. Wait till the water dries. Then put a good coat of polish all over the shoes. I usually use an old t-shirt; buff off the excess polish with a horsehair brush. Then for the magic!

"Daddy told me you buff them real good with a cloth and after you buff them then you snap the cloth. You finish up by applying a liquid polish around the soles. You do a little dance and show your customer your pride in your work. It's all a big show, but it makes the tips bigger. He told me that if I ever shine shoes for others I need to act like it's the most important job in the world. In fact, correctly shining shoes is a skill, he said." Danny grinned at the older couple.

"Now spit-shining, that takes longer and much more work. After you buff from the first coat of polish you focus on the heels and the toes. You dip a cotton ball into some water and squeeze out any excess moisture so it's damp, not dripping. Then get a little polish on the damp cotton. Next apply the polish on the toe and heel of the shoe using small circular motions.

"Then you just keep doing it again until you are satisfied with the level of shine. Use a new piece of cotton each time and remove all extra polish before applying a new coating."

"It sounds like you know what you're doing, Danny. I think we can work out a little deal, if it's OK with you. We will provide your polish and what all you need. We'll send our customers your way. You keep half of all the money you make plus you keep all of your tips. We'll give you a meal each evening. And you can get a little breakfast at the cafe next door from your tip money. After we get you into a school they'll feed you lunch. You'll have to keep sleeping upstairs but you won't have to spend any time there. You get customers coming every week and you'll make decent money."

"Sure Mr. Cosmos, but school! What are you talking about?"

"School for sure, or the deal is off!" replied Cosmos. "We'll worry about that later. I have a plan. Right now we need to get you set up and earning money. How does all this sound to you?"

"Sounds wonderful, but why are you doing all this for me?"

"Cosmos smiled and said "We're not doing anything for you, Danny. You'll be earning your own money.

"Plus, we haven't told you the whole story. We had a son, Damen. He wasn't much older than you. We tried to keep him out of the war because he was so young. He survived through the Italians and then through the Germans by hiding. After World War Two was over we thought he could come down off the mountain, out of hiding.

"That's when our own people started killing each other. They claimed he was a spy and shot him in front of us. To teach everybody a lesson, they said. That's the moment Greece was no longer our country. The Germans burned our home and our own people killed our son. Our lives were destroyed by our own people. We are so grateful to be here in America. We would be very happy to have a young man like you around here to brighten our lives. And besides you can help Karan with her English. She hasn't picked it up as quickly as I've been able to."

"Maybe she can help me learn Greek in return," Danny smiled.

"So! You want to get started today?"

"Today? Right now?" Danny stammered

"No time like the present." said Cosmos, with a twinkle in his eye.

"I have some shoe shine stuff from when I tried to shine shoes myself, but had back problems and couldn't bend over to do the job. It should still be good. You can use all that stuff starting right now.

"I think you should hang your father's flag behind your stand to let people know about it. It will help the tip."

"Nope, my father's flag stays in my bag with me."

"OK, then when you come in to work you lay the flag and the medal on that shelf next to your stand and then put them back in your bag when you go upstairs to sleep."

"OK, if you think it will help," answered Danny.

"I'll make you a sign and put the prices on it. People will have to leave their shoes here for spit shines and you get to charge more. In fact, I'll tell all my customers their shoes need to be spit shined by America's best shoe shine person. You!" Cosmos points to Danny. "You are the best, aren't you? When you don't have customers at your stand you can work on the spit shines. Just makes good business sense."

"Makes good sense to me too," smiled Danny.

Danny pulled a chair into the corner of the room and set up his shoe-shine kit.

The tinkling of the bell over the shop door alerted them.

"Oh, here's your first customer now," Cosmos said upon hearing the jingle of the bell.

"Good afternoon, Mr. Stanley, your shoes are ready. They are just like new, except they need a good polishing. Tell you what, while you're here I think you need to have them shined by the best shoe shine boy in America. He's right back there in the corner," Cosmos says. "His name's Danny. It's a new service we just started."

Cosmos remained behind the counter and was delighted as he watched Danny putting on a show of shining the customer's shoes and buffing them, whipping out and snapping the rag, followed by a small dance of pride. He felt sure Danny got a nice tip. The man would send his friends.

Five hours and ten shoe shines later, "I'm really tired," Danny complained to Cosmos. "But I have a pocket full of jingle. Thank you so much for helping me get started, Mr. Cosmos."

"You've had a good day, Danny. Now you need to go on up-stairs and get some sleep. Stay away from Buford. Before you go, I have a lesson for you. I want you to start learning Greek. Not that I care about you learning Greek in particular, but what matters is that once you learn one language it becomes easier to learn others. And I know some day you're going to do a lot of traveling somewhere. So here goes; say 'kalinihta'. That means 'good night. "Katinihta, Mr. Cosmos."

"You almost got it. Say it again."

"Kalinihta, sir." Danny began gathering up his flag and medal and stowed them in his bag. He also took some of the money from his pocket and stuffed it into the toe of a shoe that had been left for spit shine. He pushed it, along with its mate, into a corner.

"Perfect, you remember that. Tomorrow we'll work on good morning. Kalinihta, Danny."

The thought of climbing the stairs up to the apartment made Danny's stomach turn. If only Buford wouldn't be there. "Please don't let him be there," he said out loud, as he slowly made his way up. He tried the door and found it locked. He sighed a big sigh of relief and pulled out the key Buford had given him. Quietly he spread the blanket left for him on the floor of the kitchen. Sleep seemed far away, but as his mind wandered over the events of the day and his good fortune to find such a kind couple to befriend him, his eyelids began to feel heavy and he slept the sleep of the very tired.

Danny woke before daylight. He peered around, but no sign of Buford. Then he heard the loud snort of the man's snoring. "Good, he's sleeping." Danny pulled on his clothes and slipped out and down the stairs. He went past the shoe shop, which wasn't open yet, and on to the little diner. He had kept enough "jingle" on him to order a good breakfast. He was starved and gobbled up the scrambled eggs and bacon. He saved the biscuit for last, slathering it with butter and jam. He washed it all down with a second cup of coffee that he sipped slowly so he could pass more time. It still wasn't time for the Shoe Shop to open. At last the clock said 7:00 A.M. He paid for his meal and even left a small tip for the waitress.

"Kaliméra, young man," Cosmos greeted Danny as the boy walked into the shoe shop.

"Pardon?" replied a startled Danny.

"Kaliméra means good morning. Last night you learned good night. Now you learned good morning. Say it yourself."

"Kaliméra," Danny let the new word roll off his tongue.

"That was perfect. It's easy to say good morning in Greek. We are going to have many Greek friends enter the shop. When you greet people in their own language here, or where ever you travel in the world, it says you care about them. You care enough to try to learn their own language. It shows respect and good manners. Wherever you go in the world, whatever you do, you need to be always learning. Always learning language, always listening to people, always learning about everything around you.

"By the way, another new word, 'Yah soo' means hello. You had a good first day yesterday. Are you ready to go to work and earn some more money?"

"Yes, sir," Danny eagerly replied as he displayed his father's flag on the shelf. He also removed his earnings from the shoe he would be shining later. He put it in his fishing bag.

"Well, let's get started. I have some shoes to repair. You stay at your stand and I'll send you customers as they come in. We'll talk more later. There goes the bell ringing now," as the door opens.

"Good morning, my friend. Looks like you need soles and heels. Is that right? These are quality shoes you have. What about a good spit shine by the best shoe shine boy in America?"

All day long, that's the way it was. One customer after another. Cosmos had a lot of friends. And Danny made sure to greet them all in Greek. Danny's pockets started getting heavy with 'jingle.'

After dinner Cosmos said, "I've been watching you today. You are good with people. You put on a great show snapping that rag and you smile and greet everybody in Greek. You are very smart and you learn fast. Seems to me that while you are here in Chicago you need to learn all you can. Does that interest you, Danny?"

"Yes, sir. I love to read and to learn."

Cosmos smiled and replied, "Tell you what. Come in a little early before we open and we'll talk some more. Is that all right? Now you run upstairs and get some rest."

"Sure," answered Danny, "But, Mr. Cosmos, do you have a jar where I can keep my earnings? Cosmos found a jar with a lid in Karen's kitchen. "Will this do?"

"Yes sir." Keeping just enough for breakfast, Danny put all his money in the jar and handed it back to Cosmos to save for him.

"Kalinihta, Mr. Cosmos, and thanks."

"I'll hide the jar over here in this corner. Kalinihta, Danny."

Another apprehensive climb up the stairs. Once again, no one there. He settled down to sleep.

There were no curtains on the dirty kitchen window in the apartment. The first rays of the sun woke Danny each day. He washed his face and pulled on his clothes to hurry to the cafe for breakfast. He wolfed down some cereal and hurried to the shop.

"Kaliméra, Danny, did you sleep good last night?"

"Kalimera, Mr. Cosmos. Well, to be honest, I never sleep much. I always have to watch and make sure I sleep in a corner away from where Buford might stumble over me in the middle of the night."

"Danny, I am so happy that you came to us. I so enjoyed our conversation yesterday. You said yesterday you wanted to learn. Were you serious?"

"Yes, Sir. I am very serious. There is so much I don't know."

"Danny, in Greece I didn't have a shoe shop. Repairing shoes is a trade I learned from my father when I was a young man. When we arrived in the United States I couldn't teach at a university like I had done in Greece, because I had no papers with me.

"You see, we had help getting in to the United States but it was

all illegal. We weren't even in France legally. When we left Greece there was a civil war going on and there was no way to get travel papers. After we arrived in Marseille, France we were met by a group of Gypsies, who were notified to watch for us. Their language, Rumani, is very similar to Greek. We became good friends with them. They showed us how to stow away to get on a ship to the United States and then we managed to get past the immigration people when we arrived. So we had no papers. That's why I can't work at my real job. We found this vacant shoe shop with all the equipment already installed. The former proprietor left it with rent owing. So we worked out a deal with the owner of this building."

"What was your real job, Mister Cosmos?"

"Danny, I was a professor of philosophy at the University of Athens, one of the largest universities in Europe. When the Nazis came they raised their Nazi flag above the Acropolis, one of our most ancient and treasured buildings. Two of my students, Manolis Glezos and Apostolos Santas, climbed up and took down that hated flag. It was May 30, 1941. I remember it like it was yesterday. I knew the Nazis would be coming for me. Everybody knew I taught philosophy and philosophy teaches you to think for yourself. The Nazis didn't want anybody thinking for themselves, and especially taking down their symbol of hate. That's when I ran home and got Karan. We joined our son and hid in the mountains."

"Mr. Cosmos, what is philosophy?"

"Philosophy is literally the love of wisdom. My Greek ancestors started teaching it about 1500 years ago. A philosopher does not accept what others say as absolute. They always question everything. They question why the door closes in one direction and not another. They question why we use leather for shoe soles. From all that questioning comes new ideas. Sometimes those questions even cause rebellion and political revolution. That's why Socrates, one of the founders of philosophy, committed suicide. But that's a story for later.

"Right now it's time to open the shop and get to work. Do you want to come in a little early every morning so we can have time to talk?"

"Yes, sure, Mister Cosmos. I can't wait to know what happened to Socrates. But you haven't given me a word to learn today."

"That's right, I haven't. What about Efharisto? It means thank you. Now you say it."

"Efharisto."

"Very good, Danny. By the way, another bit of information. The Greek language is 4,000 years old. Two thousand years older than the Bible. You are learning ancient history with each word you learn! There goes the bell already, let's get to work." Just then somebody entered the door.

That night, though tired from a busy day, Danny found it hard to sleep. His mind was filled with images of Cosmos and Karan escaping to the mountains and then stowing away on a ship. When the sunlight fell across his eyes he could barely believe it was time to begin a new day. But the thought of finding out more about Socrates motivated him to get going.

"Kaliméra, Danny, are you ready for another good day?

"Kalimera, Mister Cosmos. You bet! I'm really anxious to hear more about Socrates!"

"Say, do you talk with your mother much?" Asked Cosmos.

"No, I haven't even seen her. She comes in late at night and is still asleep when I come downstairs. I can't wake her because Buford is always sleeping in there where she is."

"I'm so sorry, Danny. Are you ready to learn a little more?"

"Yes Sir" replied an eager Danny, glad to change to a more pleasant topic.

"OK, let me tell you the subjects you need to learn. But first I want you to know I'll help you and I'll tell you where to go look for more information. You need to take advantage of all the learning you can while you are here in Chicago.

"I already talked about philosophy. Next comes literature. Then comes math and machinery. Then art. And after that some history."

"All that?" asks Danny. "I don't know if I can learn all that."

"Yes, all that and more! Your mind is like a sponge that is hungry to be filled." Cosmos replies. "But we'll take each one in small easy bites."

"How did you learn to speak English so good?" asks Danny.

"Danny, when I was a student at the University of Athens it was a requirement for a doctoral degree to learn a foreign language. That means I am a doctor of philosophy. So I chose English. Little did I know that I would find myself in this wonderful country."

"Did you just say that you are a professor and a doctor? Should I call you doctor?"

"You heard correct, but a doctor of philosophy, not a medical doctor. Danny, most of my customers, now, were students of mine in the old country. Many of them came here to escape the Nazis and the civil war. They remember me well and that's why I have so many customers. They all call me Kathigitís. That's the Greek word for professor. Would you like to call me kathigitís also?"

"Yes, sir, I would, Kathigitis," replies Danny. "Kathigitis," the boy repeated the word, committing it to memory.

"Good pronunciation, Danny. Tomorrow I'm going to tell you about the person I think is the greatest philosopher of all time. Now let's get to work. We will have to wait to discuss Socrates until tomorrow morning, I'm afraid."

Danny crept upstairs and cautiously opened the door to the apartment as he did every night after work. This time he carried a stack of clean folded clothes. Karan had insisted he bring her his laundry, knowing that he had little time, or the means to do so on his own. He placed the clean clothing near his pallet in an out-of-the-way corner in the kitchen. Late in the night the sound of the door slamming shut and Buford stumbling about woke him. The living room light filtered into the kitchen, Buford was looking for food. Danny was afraid to breathe, but to his relief, the drunken man turned off the lights and headed to the bedroom. Danny fell into a fitful sleep.

Feeling like he hadn't been to bed at all, Danny made the trip downstairs once again. He had been very quiet and careful not to wake his snoring step-father.

"Kalimera, Kathigitis."

"Kalimera, Danny. How are you today?"

"I think something is wrong with my mother." Danny blurted out. "I never see her. She comes in late at night and is still asleep when I come downstairs. I think Buford is trying to keep her

away from me. She's got to know I'm here. I think she's afraid."

"Danny, I don't know what to say about that or how to handle it. Perhaps we can both think on that for a while. Buford is a monster. All I can promise you is Karan and I will always be here for you."

"For now," said the dark complexioned man with the curly salt-and-pepper hair, "We're going to talk about the greatest philosopher of all time, Socrates. He died about 400 years before Christ was born. Socrates was a great military commander in his early years so people respected him greatly. As he got older he sat on the steps outside the Greek senate meeting place. Young men, knowing about his military history, gathered around him regularly to listen and learn. He taught that a person should question everything and everybody. What people said, how they acted, how birds fly. Absolutely everything. Take nothing for granted just because somebody says it is so. Socrates said people learn best by asking questions, rather than listening to lectures. He said students should be encouraged to ask.

"He got into trouble with the rulers of Greece so they summoned him to appear before them in a trial of sorts. The rulers felt Socrates was encouraging rebellion by teaching them to think and question. So they demanded Socrates take back everything he said and to state that he was wrong. This was under penalty of death. Socrates stood his ground and refused. So he was given a short period of time to say bye to his friends and then to return to them. Upon his return he drank a poisonous concoction made from hemlock. The two lessons from this is he would not go back on his beliefs and that a popular way of teaching today is called the Socratic method. That's encouraging students to ask questions. And that is your lesson in philosophy.

"Well Danny, tomorrow is Sunday and we are closed. I would like to ask you to visit an art museum. They call it the Art Institute of Chicago. It's on South Michigan Avenue. Not too far to walk really. While you are there I want you to look for a certain painting. It's named 'The Gulf of Marseille.' The artist was Paul Cézanne. You may have to ask somebody for help finding it. Then I want you to find out all you can about the artist and the painting. On Monday morning I want you to tell me about it. Will you do that? Here is the ten cents it will cost to get in. I don't want you to have to spend your earnings to get an education just yet. Consider it a bonus for all the hard work you have done here in the shop."

"Yes, Kathigitis. I sure will."

"Thank you, Danny. That painting means a lot to Karan and me. That's why I want you to see it for yourself. Oh, by the way, I know you always carry your bag with you. Watch out for pickpockets and thieves. They are everywhere. Got an idea. You keep all your money in your bag. What do you think about hiding all except your tips here in the shop? That way, if you do have a problem you still have most of your money. And, of course it will always be yours. Perhaps over there under the buffing machine?"

"I think that's a good idea, Kathigitis, thank you for caring and for offering.

"Now let's get to work, Danny. Since it is Saturday we have a busy day ahead of us"

Bright and early Sunday morning Danny got ready to visit the Art Museum. He asked directions from the man at a newspaper stand and learned it was only a few blocks away. "Good," he said to himself.

As Danny walked along State Street he was amazed by the tall buildings that touched the sky, the busy rush of traffic, the people racing past in every direction, and all the noise. There must be a fire somewhere he thought, but where? People were constantly running everywhere. Nobody seemed to be taking a slow Sunday morning walk.

Finally after a few more blocks and a few turns Danny found himself at the Art Institute of Chicago. His first impression was of the beauty of the two statues of lions guarding the entrance and the American flags hanging from the huge beautiful building. Danny had never seen a building that beautiful before. Seeing the flags made him think of his daddy's flag in the bag which hung from his shoulder.

Inside he set about the lesson the professor had assigned him.

"Excuse me, ma'am, I am looking for a certain painting by Cezanne. I think it's named the Gulf of Marseilles. Can you help me?"

"Oh yes, why don't I just take you," the friendly and beautiful young woman replied. "Let's talk as we walk. This museum is such a large place. You might never find it if I don't take you. First time here?" Danny nodded yes.

"My name is Sally. What's yours?"

"I'm Danny. I've only been in Chicago a short time and don't know my way around at all. I don't know anything about art. My Greek boss told me I need to come here and see that painting and then to ask about why people should study art."

"Oh, I can help you with that," Danny, "I'm an art student at the University of Chicago. I love art. Here's your painting now. Look at the dark blue of the water surrounded by older homes. This is actually a village just outside of Marseille, France.

"Paul Cezanne's mother lived there. It's such a beautiful painting. I bet this is how your friend remembers Marseille. It's such a lovely city. A friend and I went there on vacation one time. Beautiful beaches. Friendly people. Everybody makes you feel welcome. Especially in the villages just outside Marseille where my friend and I stayed. You say your boss is Greek?"

"Yes, he was a professor of philosophy at the University of Athens. He said that he had to leave the country because of all the wars. In fact he and his wife stowed away on a ship to Marseille. He's running a shoe shop now and I shine shoes there."

"Well, Danny, that explains everything. You see. Marseille was founded by Greek sailors about 700 B.C. It's the second largest city in France and the oldest. It also has a large population of immigrants, especially Greeks and Gypsies.

"You want to know why a person should study art? Me, I study it because creating artistic designs, images, buildings, makes me feel so much closer to God. I look at the beautiful designs all around and it just brings peace to my heart. Art relaxes me. It tells me there is order in our world. When I bring out my paint brush and start applying strokes I feel it's my heart and not my hand creating those strokes.

"I see you blushing and avoiding looking at the many paintings and sculptures. I bet I know why."

"Sally, I'm so embarrassed. There's pictures and statues everywhere of naked women right out in public."

"Oh, Danny, you think you see everything. But there's a lot more

to it than that. Have you ever walked down a straight road with no curves. The entire road looks the same. That's the way it is when painting men. Just one tall very handsome man. Pretty much a straight line up and down. A woman has curves. Those curves very subtly force your eyes to move up and down and all around. The curves force your eyes to linger on the painting more. And when your eyes linger on the painting more, they appreciate the painting more. Yes, paintings of naked women are beautiful.

"Danny, I must leave you now. I need to show other people around. You're such a handsome young man and your big brown eyes see everything. I hope you learn to appreciate art and visit often. I wish you were a few years older!" Sally laughed at the red faced boy. " May I give you a kiss on the cheek before I go?"

Danny nodded his head vigorously up and down since he was at such a loss for words. Sally gave him the sweetest kiss ever and turned about to walk away.

"What a nice lady," Danny said to himself. "I love today. I love art. I love Sally. I love Marseille. I'm going to go there some day."

The day was fading. It was getting to be mid-afternoon. So Danny took a nice leisurely stroll back to the awful attic apartment on State Street, with hopes that Buford was not there. He decided to stop at the café and have a bite to eat and kill a little more time.

Bright and early Monday morning Danny went downstairs to have breakfast at the small cafe. A bowl of cereal and a piece of fruit, usually an apple or orange. That was the cheapest thing on the menu. He had only splurged once. He was saving all he could for the future.

After what seemed an eternity the professor opened his shop for the day.

"Kalimera, Kathigitis."

"Kalimera, Danny. How was your weekend?"

"Kathigitis, I had the most exciting day yesterday. I saw the painting, I learned about art, and I got a kiss from a beautiful girl."

"Danny, slow down. First, what about the art?"

"Sir, I learned that art is what you feel in your heart. It can be so many things."

"Danny, you are an artist."

"What? What do you mean?"

"Son, I've watched you work and I am always pleased when you step back to admire the shoes you spit shine. Art is almost anything that you can create and take pride in. Music, buildings, flower gardens, even spit shined shoes. You don't need to use brushes and oil paint to be an artist. To be an artist is to create something that you take great pride in.

"Now what about the beautiful girl?"

"Oh, she was the lady that was showing me around. She said she's an art student at the University of Chicago. Her name is Sally. She said I'm a handsome young man, but too young for her. Sally gave me a kiss on the cheek."

"Danny, she sounds like a nice person. But you mentioned beautiful. The one thing I want you to understand is that real beauty is in the heart, the same place art is. Not everything that people call beauty comes from the heart. What does matter is what's in the heart. That's what makes a beautiful person.

"Now, Tell me about the painting itself."

"Kathigitis, the painting was beautiful. That big bright blue bay. It makes you want to go there. Sally told me some history of Marseille and how she loves the city. She also said many Greeks have settled there."

"Danny, Karan and I loved Marseille also. That was our home for many months until the Gypsies helped us stow away on a ship to America. I am so pleased that you saw some of our past.

"Kathigitis, I'm going to go there some day."

"Enough talk. Let's get to work," Cosmos smiled with a touch of good feeling in his heart. He had taught the true meaning and essence of art.

The week flew by, shining shoes every day. Danny's money in the secret stash kept growing. Danny got by on his tips for breakfast and lunch. He ate a different Greek meal every evening.

Karan was getting better with her English with Danny's help and Danny was learning more Greek. It was a very good relationship.

Danny began to feel like maybe Chicago was to be his home. He started wondering if he had enough money for his own apartment.

He enjoyed walking to the lake with the big sandy beach on Lake Shore Drive. Danny would see people fishing off the piers and admire their catch of the day.

Every evening when Danny went upstairs he had to be very careful to stay away from Buford.

Danny always looked forward to Saturday when many friends of Cosmos came in. They were good to practice his new language on and they were all good tippers.

When Saturday morning finally arrived. Danny jumped up and grabbed his bag ready to go downstairs. But he stopped cold when he saw his mother sitting at the table drinking a cup of coffee. This was the first time he had seen her sitting up and the first time he'd been able to speak to her since he had come to Chicago four weeks ago.

"Mama, I've missed you. I was afraid to ask Buford about you!" as he rushed over to hug his mama and grab a chair to sit with her he noticed she was shaking. She took a quick look around and then spoke quietly as if afraid someone might hear her.

"Oh Danny, I love you so much. I'm so scared of Buford, but I don't know what to do. He makes me work and then he takes all the money I make. He makes me steal food for him. He keeps telling me ugly stuff about what he's going to do to you if I don't mind him. Be very quiet so you don't wake him up. He's always drunk and mean."

"Mama, where are my brothers?"

"I don't know, Danny. Buford took them somewhere back when we were in Tennessee and then came back without them. I think he sold them. I've been so upset because I'm afraid we'll never see them again. I'm scared he would do the same to you. I want so badly to leave him. But I'm terrified. He's got very mean friends everywhere and he would find me. I'd go to the police but I think they're in on it too. When I do leave I've got to do it just right. Buford doesn't know I have friends too."

"Sold them?" Danny hadn't heard much of what she said after learning Buford might have sold his brothers.

"Yes, sold them. He knows people that do that. They buy or kidnap kids and then send them off to very bad countries to be treated like slaves. I'm always afraid that if I don't steal food for Buford every night he will sell me too. See those marks on my arm. He's been drugging me. He's got me on drugs. I can't get by without those drugs. I've seen him with his friends lately. I think he's about to do the same thing to you. You've got to get away. Don't worry about me. My friends will help me."

"How does he do it, Mama?"

"Simple, really. With all his brute strength he can just knock them out with a club and then when the person wakes up they're all tied up in a truck headed heaven knows where."

Crash went Mama's chair as Buford backhanded her to the floor. Blood was flowing from her nose.

"I told you to never talk to that brat. Now you've got what's coming to you!" a very drunken Buford shouted.

"Boy, give me the money you've got in that bag. You've never paid the first penny since you've been here. It's time to pay up now," as Buford grabbed Danny's bag and turned it upside down and inside out. The flag, medal, knife, harmonica, flint stones, and fishing hooks all fell to the floor. "All you've got in here is pennies. Where's your money, Boy? I know those Greeks downstairs are paying you something."

Danny mumbled something unintelligible and quickly scooped up his entire world of belongings to put back in the bag where they belonged.

"Boy, stand up here. I want to look at you," as Buford stumbles against a wall trying to stand up.

The very alert Danny asked "What do you want to look at me for?" as he slowly edged toward the door.

"Boy, I've got plans for you," Buford shouts and reached out to grab Danny.

Avoiding those big hands, Danny ran out the door and down the stairs. Behind him he heard Buford yell and the sounds of him falling down the stairs.

Danny ran to the shoe shop and took his money from the hiding place.

"Danny, what are you doing? an anxious Cosmos saw Danny and asked.

Danny faced Cosmos and answered, "I love you and Karan. Gotta go," as he headed to the door.

"Danny, wait a minute. I know you're running from Buford. Come on back here and tell me what's going on?" Cosmos ushered Danny into the back room.

"Buford's drunk and ran me off. He stumbled down the stairs. I don't know if he got up. But I've got to get out of here."

"Where will you go? "

"I'm thinking about Marseille."

"The Gulf of Marseille" by Paul Cézanne

Chapter 10

A Close call with kidnappers

C osmos started scribbling on a piece of paper. "Here is the name and address for Greek friends at the Port of Chicago. They run a small Greek Restaurant there. Basil, the owner, has the best ouzo around. That's why everybody likes to go there. But you leave the stuff alone. Here's a little money, too.

"If you get to Marseille try to contact the Gypsies. Some of them are my friends and they will help you. Remember, Karan and I have come to love you," as both Cosmos and Karan hurriedly hugged Danny. "Go out our back door so Buford won't see you."

Danny ran out the back door and down the alley as fast as he could in case Buford had made it down the stairs.

"Going anywhere, just going," the very agitated and upset Danny thought to himself as he ran towards Lake Shore Drive and the beach. "I've got to have some time to sit and think and figure all this out," he said, talking to himself.

Sitting on a wharf at the beach was peaceful and quiet. It was too early for many people to be out. There was just the ever present background city noise. But Danny was used to that. Danny just sat there looking out over the water. Professor Cosmos had told him that Lake Michigan was over a hundred miles across and three hundred miles from the docks of south Chicago to where it connected to Lake Huron and then on to the St. Lawrence Seaway and out to the Atlantic Ocean. Danny was always excited to see the large ships on the horizon navigating both north and south. Danny remembered reading The St Lawrence Seaway was opened on April 25, 1959, not so long ago.

"Here I am again," Danny mumbled. "I thought I had a home; thought I had a family, almost got an education. Cosmos and Karan were really good to me. They taught me a lot. I enjoyed learning about philosophy. I really enjoyed the trip to the art museum. Sally was nice. And Maggie Ann was nice. Seems like a hundred years since I saw her. Grandpa was good to me. I'm so sad he hurt himself. I hope Grandpa and Grandma are better. I wish there was some place for me to go back there. But nobody had room for me."

Danny watched a bird come in for a landing on the water, then continued to talk to himself just trying to make some sense of his life to this point and what to do next. "I enjoyed living in the desert. But that wasn't really a home. Am I ever going to live anywhere or will I just be a drifter all my life, wandering here and there? So many people have been good to me. But I'm never able to stay. I'm afraid I'll never see my mother again. I'll never see my brothers again, that's for sure. There is just me. I've gotta do this on my own."

"That Buford!" Danny surprised himself by shouting out loud. "He's the problem. He's why I left Tennessee; he's why I left Arizona. And now he's why I'm leaving Chicago. Another city where I thought I was almost at home. There's no place for me in Tennessee. There's nothing in Arizona, and now I am leaving Chicago because of Buford! But where do I go and how do I get there? I have a little money, but it won't last long. I know what to do. I'll try a little planning trick Cosmos taught me about when they had to leave Greece. They put all the good memories and thoughts in the right hand and all the bad in the left hand. Two hands. One full of good thoughts. One full of bad thoughts." So Danny gathered all the memories and assigned each of them to a hand as he stood palms open. When he had exhausted all the thoughts he could, he squeezed his left hand tightly as if he were compressing all those thoughts and memories into a tight ball. Then with all the strength he had he threw the imaginary ball as far into the waters of Lake Michigan as he could. "Buford, you're out of here," Danny said as he imagined the ball sinking to the bottom of the lake.

"Now, let's see what's in my right hand of good memories and thoughts. Alabama? Some day, I hope. Arizona? No. Tennessee? No. Chicago? No, not as long as Buford is there." In the right hand Danny had placed memories of all those he loved and who had loved and guided him well to this point. He counted among those blessing his newest friends who also had been driven from their home once. The painting of Marseille by Cezanne came into his mind's eye. "I've been saying I want to go to Marseille. It's time. But how? Well, I guess I can do it the same way Cosmos and Karan did. And with the information they gave me I can do it."

Danny was familiar with the CTA bus system already. Using some of the money he had, he boarded the bus headed to the Port of Chicago, armed with the information Cosmos had given him. He planned to pay Basil a little visit.

So, after three bus changes Danny found himself standing in front of Basil's Greek Restaurant on East 95th Street, near the Port of Chicago. Danny summoned up the courage to walk inside and ask for Basil, Cosmos's friend.

"Kalimera," Danny announced when introduced to Basil as he studied this tall athletic looking man with a full beard and a deep bass voice. Cosmos had told Danny that Greeks feel beards are a sign of wisdom and manliness. Basil certainly looked it.

"Do you speak Greek?" Basil wanted to know.

"No, Sir, I learned a few words from my friend, Kathigitis Cosmos. He said you are a friend of his and I should come to see you."

"Any friend of Cosmos is certainly a friend of mine. Basil studied the boy before him. Thin as a rail and tall with a scrufty head of brown hair. But with a little food he could be handsome," Basil thought.

"Have you eaten today? Let's get some food in you and then we'll see what you need. Adrian here is our best waiter. He will give you whatever you want and don't you worry about the bill. I'll leave you alone to eat while I finish up a few things."

After about twenty minutes Basil returned to Danny, who was

still seated at a table. "How was the meal, my new young friend, and what is your name?"

"Sir, my name is Danny. Thank you for the wonderful food. It's exactly what Karan, Cosmos's wife, cooked."

Basil nodded and smiled. "Well, Danny, tell me about yourself and what I can do for you."

"Sir, I have to get away. My daddy was killed in the army in Korea. My mother is living with an awful man. He ran me off. My mother said he was going to sell me. I have nowhere to go. Cosmos told me about Marseille, France. Are you able to help me get there?"

"That's a mighty big order, my young friend. How old are you?"
"Sixteen, Sir. Does age matter?"

"No, I don't guess age matters. If Cosmos sent you to me to help you get away, then he must think you are in danger. Marseille, is it?'

'Yes, Sir. It seems to be a beautiful city. Professor Cosmos has friends there and he said they will help me. I've lived all over the country but I don't really have any family to go to.

"OK, Son, I'll help you if you're sure. Have you got any money?"
"Well, Sir, I have a few dollars. That's all."

"Danny, I will give you a little bit. But I don't have enough to help with airplane or ship passage. Only thing I know is for you

to stow-away. That's how many of us came to the United States."

"Cosmos told me about that. He said that's how he and Karan got here, also. Do you think I might be able to do that?"

"Yes, of course, Danny. But it's very dangerous. You won't know where the ship is really going or what they are carrying. And you are very young, inexperienced, and alone."

"Sir, I don't have much of a life here anyway. I don't belong anywhere, so there is no reason not to go. My life is in danger if Buford finds me. He is a really bad man. I have plenty of experience in making it on my own. I've been doing it since I was ten years old when my daddy died. I've lived in lots of different places and circumstances. So far with some luck, lots of hard work and the grace of God I have managed, and I even have a handful of good memories and blessings to show for it!"

As he spoke Danny sat up a little straighter, filled with pride and confidence at the realization of what he had accomplished for himself.

"Danny, we Greeks have studied people for thousands of years. Trust me, you have great value and you are worth much. God has simply not revealed your life plan to you yet. Trust me. He will.

"Today is Saturday. Every Saturday night we have a few friends over and we play some music. You join us. After it's all over I'll fix you a pallet here in the kitchen where you can sleep tonight. Tomorrow we'll come up with a plan for you. Tonight, you enjoy, my friend! You'll be safe here.

"My friends are bringing their music instruments in now. You sit with me. I want to show you off to my other friends. Dimitri is bringing his daughter, Helena. She's about your age. She'll want you to dance with her. You'll have a good time. Especially after you try a little ouzo."

As everybody gathered around and began singing to the lively, festive music, Danny realized how good it is to have friends. A lot of hugging, patting each other on the back, hand shaking, with many smiles and much laughter. Helena was so much fun to be with. Towards the end of the night Helena danced Danny into a corner and gave him a big kiss right on the mouth. Danny's heart beat so loud he was afraid others could hear it.

"I wish you were staying here, Danny. We could be very special friends," Helena whispered, looking up at him through thick black lashes.

Danny didn't know what to say. This was a first experience for him. He thought of Maggie Ann. Finally he muttered, "But I must go."

Danny slept good that night on his pallet in the kitchen. Greek people were all so friendly and a lot of fun to be with. He fell asleep thinking of Helena and Maggie Ann and hearing the many different sounds of ships horns. He felt great adventures were about to happen.

"Kalimera, my young friend," boomed Basil's deep rich voice. "Danny, we usually have some pastries and cold cuts for breakfast. Do you want Greek or American coffee?"

"Kalimera, Sir. I've gotten to like Greek coffee. It seems to be so much more full and rich. Thank you for breakfast and for your wonderful hospitality. Could I repay your hospitality by shining your shoes or cleaning up somewhere? I'll be more than happy to."

"Danny, don't worrying about repaying me. We are all very happy for you to be here. You are our guest. We have a lot to discuss. Several of my friends here last night work for the Port Authority. But I didn't want to say anything or ask for help for fear they might slip something or try to stop you. I guess you can do what we did when we left Greece. Just watch for the ship's flag. A French flag means it's registered in France but it does not necessarily mean that's where the ship is going. Do you know what a French flag looks like? It has the same colors as the American flag, but reversed and has vertical stripes. Blue, white, and red. Look for a ship that doesn't seem as well maintained. Their security might be lax too.

"You can run into trouble when you don't really know what is on the ship or what the crew is like. Some things to look for are whether the ship is riding high in the water or low. If it's riding high that means the ship has off-loaded its cargo and is awaiting to be loaded. I would look for such a ship and then watch for it to be loaded. After it's loaded you will see sailors boarding. You might be able to sneak in among them. You'd just have to act like you know what you're doing and to be very casual about it. Be sure to get out of that line as quick as you safely can, because you don't know where they are headed.

"You can't go looking around like a tourist. Carry a bag of stuff like it's your gear and walk aboard with a steady but determined gait. Take plenty of food and water. You're looking at about a two week trip. And the North Atlantic gets cold, even in the summer time, so wear some warm clothing. I can help with that. I have an old bag here you can have. You can put your other stuff in it, too.

"The moment you get aboard start looking for a hiding place. Then do your best to stay out of sight. Never look anybody in the eye. Always look down and act like you're a nobody. A person can only go for about 3 days without water so you are going to have to move about a little bit. You will also need to find a bathroom occasionally; that is hard to do. So when you do have to move about always pretend to be busy, sweeping or mopping a floor or wiping down a railing. Always keep moving. Never stop to look about.

"There are some ships in the harbor now. Why don't you casually stroll down there and see what you can learn. Just make sure you keep your distance and act like a regular tourist. Now finish up that breakfast and your coffee. You need to go sight-seeing."

Danny hurried to finish his breakfast and spent the afternoon observing the docks, at a distance, being careful not to look conspicuous. Just sightseeing, he would say if asked.

When he returned to Basil's, Danny was excited to share his discoveries with him. "I'm back, Sir. Wait till you hear what I saw." "Yes, Danny, what did you learn?" Basil grinned at the excited boy.

"Basil, there's an older ship alongside a dock that is flying the

French flag. It's not the biggest ship and is kinda rusty and needs paint. It looks like they might be loading grain into it. There's a big pipe pouring something into it."

"They are probably loading grain that's been shipped here from out west. The United States is a big grain exporter.

"Danny, maybe you are in luck! Sailors will probably start boarding that ship about dark. I imagine they'll be leaving almost immediately. Some ship captains feel they can have an easier time with customs and all that paperwork if they leave by night. I'm not so sure that is true. But some of them do think that.

"I have to warn you. That's exactly the type of ship that unscrupulous sea captains would have. So you'll really have to watch out.

"Just an idea, Danny, based on my limited knowledge. That ship might be going anywhere in the world. Although I would guess it would at least stop off in Marseille because that's the biggest port in the Mediterranean. And going by way of Marseille allows them opportunity to go to many more ports on eastward.

"You will first know where you are headed if you go through the Straits of Gibraltar. It's a very narrow passage way between the Atlantic and the Mediterranean. Only about seven nautical miles. And a person can see about twenty miles before the horizon starts curving. So you'll be able to see Africa and Europe at the same time by looking right and left. You will be able to see the shores of Morocco in Africa to your right and the Rock of Gibraltar in Europe to your left. If that happens you will be about two more days to Marseille.

"If God is with you the ship will put in at Marseille. If not, life will get much more dangerous very quickly, because there's no telling which African countries they might be visiting.

"If you approach land and see white cliffs on your left you are going past England and may end up in Amsterdam. That's very likely also. And perhaps not quite as dangerous. But there are rumors of much drug trafficking and crime there.

"I'll go get you that bag so you can start loading your food, canteens of water, and other personal stuff. Just make sure you get there before they leave. You may have to go early and hide out of sight. You'll have to wait till dark and then slip down that way."

"Thank you, Sir. You have been so good to me. How will I ever repay you and Cosmos?"

"Don't you worry about repayment, my son. We'll pray for you."

At dusk Danny was packed and loaded. He wore old clothers and a flat seaman's cap to help blend in while carrying a seaman's bag hanging from his shoulder.. He practiced walking bent over and tired, however the heavy bag on his back made it easy. Just another long trip at sea, he kept repeating to himself. And with eyes darting surreptitiously in every direction.

Shortly after finding a look-out place he spotted the line of seamen. Not very many. But maybe enough to blend in. Danny began walking like he had practiced. A couple of them mumbled something to him. Danny just nodded and mumbled back like he belonged there and had been doing this for years.

Finally he was aboard and looking for a place to drop out of the line and hide. Then he saw it. As the line went around the corner he quickly slipped behind a door and stood very motionless and quiet. Finally the entire line passed. Stealthily, Danny began looking for a better place to hide. He found one and quickly ducked in. After just a few hours he heard the ship's loud, harsh horn that announced to all around that it was about to depart.

Almost immediately he felt the increased rocking of the ship. They were underway. Basil had told him Lake Michigan is well known for its storms so Danny braced for the worst. According to Basil it would be four or five days until the ship went through the St. Lawrence Seaway and out into the Atlantic.

Danny could see light through the cracks in the door so he could tell if it was night or day. He decided to count the days so he could judge how close to their destination they were. At the end of the first full day in Lake Michigan he began to hear a lot of ship traffic. Basil had also told him about going past the Merimac dock and then to Lake Huron and into the St. Lawrence Seaway. So another leg on the journey was about to begin.

The ship would pass through many locks and take several days depending on how much traffic there was. The ship would be stopped more than it would move. The life of a seaman requires patience, Danny had been told. "And," Danny says to himself, "I'm not even a seaman, just an already hungry stowaway."

After five days they were finally out in the Atlantic. Cold blustery winds and heavy rocking. "Gotta breathe fresh air to keep from being sick," Danny thought.

Then it happened. Danny was in his hiding place where he tried to stay most of the time, when the door was opened.

"Hey, what are you doing here?" a surprised voice asked.

"Kalimera," replied Danny, hoping to confuse the intruder with another language since the question had been in English.
"Oh, are you Greek" the intruder asked.

"No, Sir," Danny knew the ruse didn't work. He had been found out. Danny frantically searched his brain for something to say that would account for his being there but nothing came to him. In the end he just went with telling the truth. "But I have Greek friends."

"You do? Who? Where? The intruder demanded.

"Sir, my very good friend is Professor Cosmos who taught philosophy at the University of Athens. He is like a father to me."

"Is he the one whose students were caught taking down the Nazi flag? He's a hero in our country. What's he doing now?"

"Sir, he and his wife, Karan, run a small shoe repair shop in Chicago. I needed help so they took me in and told me their story of stowing away to Marseille and then to the United States, to get away from all the wars in Greece. That's when I learned how special Greek people are."

"What is your name and where are you from? Where are you hoping to go?"

"Sir, my name is Danny. I got on this ship in Chicago. I'm hoping to go to Marseille because it seems to be so beautiful and the Professor gave me names of his friends there."

"Danny, my name is Alessandro. I also went to the University of Athens and had trouble with the law, so I managed to get away. I went to Marseille and then to Chicago. But then I had more trouble. The people that run this ship are very bad. I will do everything I can to help you. But you're really going to have to watch out."

"Alessandro, why do you say the people are so bad?

"Danny, this ship isn't really shipping grain. You see, the St. Lawrence Seaway was just opened a couple of months ago allowing ships to go all the way from Chicago to Europe. So a few evil people felt the customs and immigration would be over burdened with a huge backlog of ships trying to get through. What some of them did was go buy cheap ships and build false bottoms in them and then pretend they are shipping grain. They ask the grain people to only put in enough grain to cover the upper hold and then falsify the shipping documents. The lower hold is full of people."

"People! I don't understand," suddenly images of Danny's brothers filled his mind and he understood.

"Yes, human beings. You see, along the northern coast of Africa the tribes are always at war with each other. So they pay good money for people to help them fight. Many of their soldiers are barely out of diapers. A few of the people die on the way over but they feel that's a small loss because there are so many all packed in there. They pay good money in the United States and all over, to kidnappers," Alessandro explained.

"I think we're stopping off briefly in Marseille. I'll tell you more later. I've got to go now. Just stay right here. Don't get caught or your life is over. I'll bring you some food and water when I can slip away again."

Three days later Danny began to feel cramped, starved, dehydrated, and cold. It was almost too much for him to handle.

Alessandro opened the door to a startled and scared Danny.

"Very sorry I've been so long. While we're traveling through the St. Lawrence Seaway the first mate has deck hands everywhere. They are so afraid something might go wrong while we're going through the locks. Here, I brought you some water and some food. From the smell in here I think maybe you need to visit the head, that's what we call a bathroom. Tell you what, take my jacket and cap so you can look like me. We're almost the same build. Walk out of this closet to your left and go a short distance. You'll see the head on your right. When you come back be sure to look about to make sure nobody is watching."

"Thank you, Alessandro. I was really beginning to worry."

"Danny, when you get back we can talk more about what to expect. Let me peek out the door to see if it's safe. You're OK. Now go! Take your time."

Danny acted like he belonged on board sweeping the floors, or decks, as he had heard them called. Never looking anybody in the eye. Never standing still, always busy.

Danny arrived back and quickly entered the small closet "That's a relief. Thank you, Alessandro. What do you think about our journey?"

"Danny, figure about ten days or so depending on the speed they set. Most captains take a northerly route. This is July so that means for a couple of nights it just might look like daylight outside, depending on how far north we go. The North Atlantic will be cold always and maybe rough, depending on storms.

"We're headed into storm season. That's when the hot winds of the Sahara kick up and start traveling all the way across the Atlantic blowing up storms and hurricanes all along the way. The Sahara Desert is so big that the entire United States, twice over almost, can fit in it. When all that sand heats up in their very hot summer, it causes turbulence and people get hit by storms of all kinds, all around the world. So let's hope for the best."

"How do you know so much about the weather and the Sahara Desert, Alessandro?"

"I'm Greek. We are all sons and daughters of the Sahara. I've been gone too long and have to go now. I'll be back as soon as I can. Hang in there, American."

Two nights later Danny slipped out very carefully and made it to the head and back. Although he was very thirsty, once again, he was scared about drinking the faucet water in the head. He had heard that sometimes ships reprocess their water. He had almost run out of the water Allessandro had brought him.

A night later Danny cracked open the door and saw that although there was no sun out it was as bright as daylight. Sailors were all out milling about watching the strange sight so Danny quietly closed the door. He had read about the Aurora Borealis once. The red and green formations in the sky were what the crew was watching.

Finally, two days later, night took over again. Danny figured the ship had reached its northernmost point and was headed in a southerly direction again.

Alessandro slowly opened the door. "Anybody home, American?" he said softly.

"Right here, Greek. Thought about going swimming but forgot my swim trunks."

"You Americans, you're always making fun. Good news! I've overheard people talking. It looks like in two more days or so we'll be headed through the Straits of Gibraltar. So we really will make it, I hope. That's when you and I need to make plans for getting off this tub."

"Both of us?"

"Yes, Danny, they'll want to sell me too. I've heard too much talk. They are very greedy. Every drachma counts. Dollars, drachma, lira, marks, whatever they can get. And they, for sure, will sell you as soon as they find you. But don't you worry about it. Marseille is really a Greek Port. I think I can get us some help. But we'll have to be careful. Let me think on it some more. We'll talk details next time I come."

As they slowly navigated through the very narrow Straits of Gibraltar Danny could sneak a look up on his left side and see the quarter mile high Rock of Gibraltar, just as he had been told.

On the right he knew the Morocco ports were close and very busy. Danny knew he was entering the Mediterranean. Danny wanted to get out and watch the sight, but he knew it was very dangerous if he didn't stay out of sight. Only about two days to go. He wished Alessandro would hurry and come visit him, but he knew Alessandro was scared of being caught because of so many people on deck during the Straits navigation. People and ships everywhere. It was such a busy place.

Finally, a day later. Alessandro came. "Danny, here's food and water. I think we will be approaching Marseille tomorrow evening. So here's what I think will happen. They will try to unload the grain about dusk when customs agents won't be able to see so much. The ship will head straight in to the dock. They will probably put a big pipe on the port side, that's the left side. If that happens everybody will be on that side watching to make sure everything is hooked up correctly. That's when we slip out on the starboard side, the right side, the side we're on. You'll have to carry only what you just absolutely have to have or else you'll probably sink.

"I'll try to slip you a life ring earlier in the day. Then about dusk I'll come for you. You'll have to be ready to run and hit the side to jump in the water. I'll be right next to you. There will probably not be another ship right next to us. This captain won't like berthing next to other ships. After you hit the water swim just as fast as you can for the big pilings that support the docks. Once you get there hide behind it, pause and catch your breath. I'll be right beside you all the way. You can swim can't you? If not our goose may be cooked!

"Once we get under the dock we will have to look to see if anybody on the dock is watching. If not we can swim straight in. Otherwise we may have to swim past some docks. That could be dangerous because any big ships coming in won't be able to see us. We might have to wait right there until it gets a little darker."

"My Greek friend, I can swim and if I had swim trunks I'd put them on right now and get ready, I am so tired of this closet." a scared Danny replied while trying to act cheerful. Danny spent the rest of the evening and the next day nervously waiting and trying to rest. Every time he heard noises on the deck he tensed up ready to jump.

At last the door opened. Alessandro excitedly whispered, "Let's go!"

They both ran and jumped, the noise from the splash was drowned by the sounds of shouts and the din of the engine. Danny, with only his fishing bag and a life ring, and Alessandro with even less. Was this certain death or freedom? They were about to learn as they furiously kicked and paddled towards the big pilings and out of sight, terrified to look back. Danny struggled with his bag, afraid he might lose it, even while the bag kept dragging him down deeper in the chilly water. Danny was a good swimmer because he swam a lot in the creek where he and his daddy fished. But he knew he wouldn't drown in the creek. This was much different.

Every noise from every direction made them kick even harder. It could be slavery, forced battles, and then an awful death. If they were fast enough it might all be behind them.

"Danny, I think we made it. Careful now, you stay out of sight.

 I'll sneak a quick peek and see if anybody's about and if they saw us.

"I don't see anybody around. They didn't see us. But it's still just a little bit light out. Why don't we rest up right here while it gets a little darker? It'll be a lot safer, " Alessandro advised.

"Let's be very quiet, though, just in case." The two young men clung to the huge posts, the deep water swelling, and ebbing. An hour or so later, Alessandro suggested, "Danny, everything seems to be quieted down and hardly anybody moving about, and it's good and dark. I don't think they have even missed me. Why don't we very slowly and quietly move from one piling at a time towards the dock. Let's stop at each one to look back to check. Oh, and you need to tie that life ring under here. Someone might spot it."

"Whatever you say, Greek. You're the captain here. I'm right behind you."

One at a time they slowly made their way to shore, careful lest someone be alerted to the presence of two former stow-aways who were illegally entering France. They knew they would never see day light again if they were caught.

One more piling and they would be ashore. Alessandro whispered, "I still don't see anyone. Let's head for that building. He pointed in the direction of a run-down structure. There are no lights on. Don't run, that might alert somebody. Just kinda saunter like a seaman would. We'll have to be careful not to set off any alarms. When we get there lie on the ground in the shadows till our clothes dry. On the way, if you hear any noise, hit the ground and flatten yourself and hope nobody will see you."

The two boys stealthily made their way into the shadow of the old building. They watched as the glittering lights were gradually extinguished. A little later most businesses were closed on the nearby streets. Only a few bars remained open. There were always bars near a dock looking for thirsty sailor's money.

"Tell you what, American. You wait here. Most everybody here is Greek. Let me go and see what I can find for us. Hide in this corner. The Gendarmes might be around any moment looking for villains like us."

"Hiding again," Danny said to himself, as he watched Alessandro slowly walking away, looking like he belonged there. At least they were finally on dry land and safer, but he sure didn't feel secure yet. Danny began to wonder if he had really been wise to choose this path. For the first time since he had left Grandma and Grandpa's house, Danny bowed his head and whispered a prayer. He asked God for the safe return of his new Greek friend and guidance for the way ahead. Then he listened intently for the approach of footsteps.

Chapter 11

Gypsy Camp in Marseille, France

anny, I'm back! We're in great luck. There's a Gypsy camp about a kilometer from here. I talked with their head man and they'll take us in. When I told him you have American dollars his eyes lit up. So here's what we do. We start wandering down the street here and acting a little drunk. Not too much or the Gendarme will pick us up. We just want to be happy drunks. If anybody speaks just mumble. Everybody speaks Greek here so I'll answer if I have to. Again, don't look anybody in the eyes. You still got your fishing bag? Good, let's go."

Danny didn't know much about being drunk so he watched others around him and tried to do the same, as he faked his stumbling on down the street. When they approached the Gypsy camp Danny noticed it had become very dark. There were no lights in this part of town. Fifteen minutes or so of stumbling and then Alessandro pushed Danny to turn to the right into some woods bordering a garbage dump. "So that's what I've been smelling.

I thought it was you," Danny joked.

"Oh you American!" Alessandro chided, grinning.

Standing in front of a small campfire several people were waiting for them to arrive. "Welcome boys. I'm Dominick, the Rom Baro, the leader of our small clan. We open our hearts and all we have to you, what little we have, that is. We are a very small clan and very poor. But first stand in front of the fire here and let me look at you.

"You're nothing but skin and bones! When's the last time you've eaten? What's your name?" the Rom Baro asked Danny.

"Sir, I haven't eaten in two days, food was hard to come by on the ship. That's where Alessandro and I met. He helped me get here and truly saved my life. My name is Danny, and my friend in the United States said that Gypsies helped him and his wife escape Greece years ago and that I can trust and depend on them to help me in the same way."

"Well, Danny, my English is not the best. But we'll get along. We need to sit here and talk a little.

"Dimitri, go get Danny and Alessandro a bowl of that soup we have left over," Dom ordered the man standing closest to him by the fire.

Danny found a place to sit on an old board and asked, "Are we safe here? If we're caught we'll be sold as slaves, if they don't kill us. I have no passport. But I do have a few American dollars. What do we need to do?"

"Danny, yes, you are safe here. Nobody cares about us Gypsies. They don't offer us food yet they won't let us work. They won't let us live anywhere decent. So we mostly live in places where they wouldn't imagine living; near the garbage dumps. Much of our food comes from garbage cans behind restaurants. We eat the food that people leave on their plates and scrape into the garbage. Three of our men go searching every night for food.

"You're in luck. We have some grape seeds that we have roasted to make coffee with. So you'll have some coffee in the morning, or would you like some right now?"

"Sir, we've had a very long day and am very tired. Is there a place we can just go to sleep?"

"Yes," Dominick replied "There's a corner over here near where I sleep. Here's a couple of blankets for your beds. Fortunately you are in Marseille in the middle of July, so you'll be warm. We may have a few rain showers, though. Not much I can do about that. Watch that rats don't get at your bag. Good night."

"Good night, Sir"

"Oh, Danny, don't call me Sir. I'm their leader but everybody just

calls me Dom. Good night, Danny."

Danny slept fairly sound that night, using his bag as a pillow. Even on the hard ground, as a gentle rain fell, he barely stirred. Occasionally, he felt movement across his body, but just slapped it away.

A deep voice boomed, "Good morning." Danny opened one eye to see Dom standing over him. He offered Danny a chipped cup filled with a dark steaming liquid. "Here's what I call coffee," he said to Danny. "Hope you slept the night. The coffee is made from roasted grape seed, not so good, but it's the best we can offer. Now tell me what's in that bag you are holding on to so tightly." Meanwhile, Alessandro took the cup offered him and wandered about the camp, talking to the other Gypsies as they began their day.

Danny sat up and slowly pulled out the contents of his bag, and explained them. "This is my harmonica. My daddy taught me how to play it. This is my daddy's flag from the Missing In Action Memorial Service they held for him after the war in Korea." Danny unwrapped the flag to show Dom. He had wrapped it in a piece of oil cloth from Basil's restaurant but it felt damp. He would let it dry soon.

"He served here in Europe in World War Two and later went to Korea. And this is the hero medal President Eisenhower gave him for saving lives in Korea. The rest of it is my knife, some fish hooks and line, some fire starter rocks, and my American dollars."

"Danny, you are a boy full of mysteries. Will you play that harmonica for us? Some lively music might be just the thing to lift the spirits of our little rag-tag clan today!"

"Sure, I can. What would you like to hear? I can play almost anything?"

"How about some jazz?"

Danny had to think a moment about that and finally settled on a lively polka he had heard once. He placed the harmonica to his lips and began to breathe and blow out a happy tune. When he looked up a few people had gathered around him to listen and several were smiling at him as he played. "How's that, Dom?"

"Danny, you can earn some good money for all of us with your playing. But first, let's talk about your daddy when he was here in Europe. All Gypsies owe World War Two American Soldiers a huge debt of gratitude.

"You see, when Hitler was rounding up the Jews he was also rounding up Gypsies. Nobody kept exact numbers but people estimate that over 200,000 Gypsies were sent to the gas chambers. Most of us are alive today only because of America. The holocaust wasn't just about the Jewish people. Millions of people from across Europe were rounded up and exterminated.

"Your flag looks a little wet. You must take good care of it. Here, take it out and spread it across these boards in the sunshine. My people will watch and take care of it. They have much respect for it. Now play me another song on your harmonica."

After spreading his flag to dry, Danny played a slow mournful gospel tune. Everybody gathered around and started singing the words of an old Gypsy song, to the tune he played. Danny had accidentally hit upon the right song. When Danny finished they all applauded and started away. They had a full day of work to do. "Where's everybody going, Dom?"

"Danny, everybody here has a job. Our younger boys have garbage cans they check on every morning. Some of our kids go to the fish market looking for throwaways. Others just wander the streets looking for anything of value. Maybe a piece of tin or a board. We can use everything."

"Dom, I understand that! When I lived in the desert I had to make use of anything and everything I could find to live, on a daily basis. Maybe I was part Gypsy in my life too. Tell me more about you and your people."

"We think our people originally came from India about 1300 years ago. You see, India has what they call a caste system. Depending on what family you are born into you might be of the very top caste, or the very bottom. The very bottom group are called 'unclean.' Nobody really knows why, perhaps because they are so poor they don't have the means to keep clean. Our people wanted to break away from that unfair system so we started spreading north and across Europe. At first people thought we came from Egypt. That's where the name 'Gypsies' came from.

"We call ourselves Romani. That's our correct name. All our clans are made up of family groups. We strongly believe in family, and we believe in sticking together as a people. Lots of people run us off because they say we steal. We would rather not steal. We just try to get by."

"So your title 'Rom Baro' means something like 'Romani Leader'?" Danny asked.

"Yes, it does. We leaders are not really bosses like you would think. But we are responsible for the security and welfare of our clan."

"Well then, I will start saying Romani. Are there other Romani clans?"

"Danny, yes, there are many clans. Some of our our clans do get together at times. That's when the leaders and elders sit and talk about the old ways. Our young people enjoy the dancing and the music. By doing that we have Romani friends across all of Europe, even into the Soviet Union. All the countries try to ignore us like we don't exist. We are a problem to them. A blemish on their society."

"Dom, You said I could make you some money. What do you mean?"

"Good question, Danny. Romani are known for the music we make. In fact most music from across Europe and America started with the Romani. You see, back about the year 1400 the church felt it was hypocrisy to play music. So people hired us to make music for them. Then as the church started easing up, the people began playing what they had learned from us.

"Now then, how can you make money and help us? Danny, although we are known for our music only a few of us know how play well. Whenever we are lucky enough to play for somebody we have to gather up musicians from several clans. And then the money has to be split among everybody. We don't have any musicians in our clan.

"If you're alright with it, what I'd like to do is get one of our people, Dimitri perhaps, to take you to a street corner where you can simply sit and play your harmonica. Dimitri will help watch out for the Gendarme and other people that might bother you. You just put a hat out in front of you and smile at everybody while you are playing. You keep half the money for yourself, the other for us. Will you do that?"

"Sure, Dom, whatever I can do to help. I'll try my best to make you some good money to repay and thank you for all your kindness and trouble. I'd like to do some sightseeing while I'm here, too. There's a place called 'Gulf of Marseille'. I saw a painting of it when I was in Chicago, by a French painter named Cezanne. I'd like to go there and see the real gulf for myself. I'd also like to go to Paris, Florence, Italy, and then behind the Iron Curtain - the Soviet Union."

"Sounds like we have a bargain then, Danny. Let's see how much money you can bring us this evening, and I will try to find a way for you to begin to see some of the places you named."

"Dimitri, you take Danny and get him started. While you're at it see if you can convert all his dollars to francs."

When Danny and Dimitri returned to the Gypsy camp that evening, Danny heard a strong and beautiful voice singing a lively song, but no instruments accompanied her. It was dusk and the campfire glowed and crackled while a few women dancers twirled about, their colorful skirts whirling and cheap bangles glinting in the firelight. Others stood by clapping to create the rhythm. There was excited talk and laughter. Dom and some of the men were taking stock of the day's treasures. Danny sat down and added his harmonica to the beautiful voice. It was like magic. Once again Danny had that wonderful feeling of belonging but he pushed it down deep in his soul knowing full well that whenever he began to feel safe something happened. Little did he know how right he was.

Suddenly gun shots shattered the gathering. Whistles were blowing. Bull horns pierced the night. Gendarmes and belligerent sailors burst into the camp. Chaos erupted; women screaming, children running and the men being knocked down by the intruders. Mass confusion everywhere.

"Where is he? Where are you hiding him?" The ship's captain demanded. "Alessandro, I know you are here! You'd better get over here now, or I'm going to flog and keelhaul you. Nobody deserts my ship!" The first mate with a bull horn and his sailor thugs were knocking everybody down. "Anybody helping him is going to get the same treatment. Get out here right now or I'm going to burn this whole sewage pit down. You cost me another whole day of port charges."

"Alessandro, you heard the man, get out here right now," shouted the Gendarme captain through a bull horn.

The Rom Baro had quickly herded Danny, Dimitri, and Alessandro into a hiding place, while the intruders searched, destroying the meager shelters as they went. "Danny, you give me some of your money, hurry! All of you wait right here and stay hidden." Trusting Dom completely, Danny quickly gave him a handful of the francs he had earned that day.

Dom ran toward the Gendarme captain. He whirled and faced the man with the bull horn. Leaning close to the man's ear, Dom whispered something. He slipped some francs into the man's hand. A few moments later they heard the Gendarme captain shouting in his bull horn "Let's go. They're not here. Everybody out! We'll look somewhere else." Within moments the camp was cleared of the hateful intruders.

When it was safe, Dom went to the small cave in the woods where he had hidden the three people. They know you are here. They'll be back without the Gendarmes and they'll be a lot meaner. "

Chapter 12

Panhandling in Paris, France

Dimitri, you take Danny to your friend who drives the shrimp truck. He'll be leaving any time now to get to Paris in time for the daily fish market to open. Go through Thieves Alley. Gendarmes won't go there and strangers know to stay away, but the people there know you.

"Keep Danny in Paris for a week. Make sure he does some sight-seeing after he has made us some money by playing his harmonica on the streets of Paris. Then bring him back home. Maybe with a lot of tourist money."

"I'll take care of him, Dom. I'll make sure he enjoys Paris also." Dimitri replied.

"Danny, you got your bag and all your stuff? You hang on to that harmonica. That and your skills are worth a lot of money," ordered the Rom Baro.

"Bemus, take Alessandro to the Greek olive oil merchants. He'll fit in there and they'll take care of him. About now they'll be getting their olive oil ready to ship out. Take Alessandro through the cemetery. Nobody goes that way at night.

"The rest of us will be alright, because when they come back we will be very courteous and polite. We will open everything to them. The Gendarmes were ready to take any amount of money because it's all about the money to them. They know these thugs will be sailing soon. But we need to get you two out right now because as soon as they are out of Gendarme sight they will return."

Danny turned to Alessandro and told him "I'll probably never see you again. Thank you so much for being there when I really needed help. You saved my life and I will never forget you. Now let's get out of here. Be safe, my friend."

Alessandro turned to Danny and gave him a big hug."Good-bye, American."

As Danny ran down the road following Dimitri he recalled Dom's words. "Bring him back home," Dom had said. Did he mean it? Did he really feel that Dom's clan was home for Danny?

"Let's go to Paris," Dimitri said. "I guess you never been there?"

"No, I haven't. Don't know anything about it or how we're going. Can you please tell me?"

"Well, Danny, you're in luck. I've spent a lot of time in Paris. My shrimp trucking friends often take me along as an extra driver. I stay a few days, look around a little bit, and then catch a ride back home with them. That is what we'll do now."

When they reached town they kept to the darkened streets and alley ways. Danny paid particular attention to how Dimitri moved through the streets and used the shadows to cross streets and often ducked around corners when groups of people appeared in their path. Then he would check in all directions before beginning to move forward again. After about 20 minutes of cutting back and forth through streets and alleys the two travelers came to an open parking area just opposite several small docks.

"Here we are and there's our driver, Max, and his truck. Let's get in. "Bonsoir, mon ami. Comment allez vou? Merci, je vais bien. C'est mon ami, Danny."

"Danny say 'bonsoir'. That means good evening. Max doesn't speak English. You're going to learn a lot of other languages very quick. But I will help." He went on to ask Max if they could hitch a ride to Paris with him.

"O oui! oui!" smiled Max, apparently glad for the company. He motioned for Danny and Dimitri to climb up into the spacious front of the truck, the back of which, at the moment, was being filled with what looked like enough shrimp to feed the entire town. The tires on the truck began to smoosh slightly as they took on the weight of the load. Danny climbed in first and Dimitri took the window seat. Once the rear of the truck had been fully loaded and secured Max joined them in the driver's seat and started the engine with a roar. The three settled in for the trip and Dimitri began to tell Danny more about what lay ahead.

Although Dimitri spoke with a heavy accent, he spoke English very well. "We are in for about an eight hour drive. The auto route we're taking, A7, was actually built by the Nazis in World War Two. The Germans built major highways to help move their troops quickly from one place to another. Your President Eisenhower started the highway interstate system in America for exactly the same reason. Other things you'll see are the international road signs. Once you see them for a while they get to be pretty easy to learn. But I doubt you'll be driving, anyway.

"We measure distance in kilometers in Europe. It's pretty easy really. You Americans use the old English system of feet, yards, and miles, depending on whatever size the English king's foot was. Here we are metric. Everything is in tenths, just like your dollars. Millimeter, centimeter, kilometer. A thousandth part of a meter, a hundredth part of a meter and a thousand meters. A meter is the main measuring unit. Each one is times ten. Distances are usually in kilometers. One kilometer is sixty-two hundreds of a mile. A little over a half a mile.

"You'll catch on pretty quick. It's kinda fun, really. Look over at the speedometer. See that it reads 120. Fast, huh? In miles, we are only going about seventy five miles an hour."

Danny listened intently as Dimitri spoke, "Every country in Europe uses their own currency, French Francs, German Marks, Swiss Francs, Italian Lira, English Pounds. Seems to me they need to get together. All I know is every time I have ever crossed a border I lost money in the exchange. The exchange rate is always in the other person's favor.

"Danny, I've been doing a lot of talking, but I know nothing about you. Looks like we're going to spend a few days together. Tell me about yourself and what brings you to this part of the world."

"Dimitri, I am enjoying learning from you and I hope you will tell me much more. You seem very knowledgeable.

"As for my story, my daddy fought in World War Two here in Europe and then again in Korea where he died a hero. My mama started going out with lot of men. The last one was very mean. I think he sold my younger brothers and I was afraid he was going to sell me. So I've had no home for several years now. I worked for a very nice Greek couple shining shoes in their shoe repair shop in Chicago. They told me how beautiful Marseille is and here I am."

"Danny, I apologize for interrupting you, but I want to tell you we are driving through Avignon right now. You can see the signs alongside the road. Most people think the Pope of the Catholic Church has always lived in The Vatican in Rome, but that's not the case.

"In the early 1300's King Phillip IV of France actually arrested the Pope and cruelly tortured him. After he died Phillip forced the papal conclave in Rome to vote for Clement, a French cardinal. As Phillip expected, Pope Clement refused to move to Rome. So he took the Papacy to Avignon where the Catholic popes lived for almost seventy years. Finally after a lot of upheaval inside the Catholic church the pope, or the papacy as they call it, moved back to The Vatican in Rome, where it is today."

Danny's eyes grew big as they drove past the ancient buildings illuminated by the street lights, some of them hundreds and hundreds of years old. He had never seen anything so old, not in Rattlesnake Cove, Chicago, or even Tucson. He yearned to be able to stop and explore the ancient buildings, but there was no time now. The ruins quickly faded as they sped down the highway and the scenery quickly turned to farm land and vineyards. It was after midnight but he could see some of the land because of the occasional car lights.

"Well, Danny, we have several hours. Max will stop about half way there for a bathroom break. So you may as well close your eyes and sleep a little bit. That's what I'm going to do."

As they sped on Danny tried to sleep, but he was too excited. His thoughts were all over the place. First he went over in his head the information that Dimitri had just given him, the history, the metric system and the monetary system in this new place; next the thought of President Eisenhower and the roads he built in America; lastly his thoughts turned to his father and how he had saved lives.

He hoped he would be as good a man as his father. Danny remembered that one time Daddy had said, "Son, wherever you go, whatever you do, somebody is always watching. Yes, I know it may seem ugly. But think about it for a moment. People talk about people. I call it gossip, but I hear it all the time. What really matters is that everything you do you must set an example for others. You must show them that what you are doing is the right thing to do. People need other people to look up to these days. They need to see people who are living their lives right and always helping others. I want you to be that kind of man."

Yes, Daddy was always telling him how to live a good life and to help others. "I'm going to be the man my father wanted me to be." Danny said to himself.

Danny's mind then wandered to other places. "How did his mama ever get mixed up with a man like Buford? One bad person can shatter a lot of lives," he thought.

"I need to stop all that ugly thinking. After my dad, I've had a lot of good people helping me. There was Cosmos and Karan. Cosmos is a great man. He's the one who first told me about Marseille and he taught me about ancient Greek history. Maybe I can go there some day," Danny reminisced.

"And then there was Basil, and Alessandro. And especially my grandparents in Rattlesnake Cove, Alabama. I'm going back there someday to Maggie Ann. She's the one sweet moment in my life. But her parents and her brother are characters," Danny laughed to himself. Danny's mind started fading away to a peaceful sleep as they continued the long ride.

"Danny, wake up! Max is stopping for fuel and bathroom. Do you need to go?" Dimitri was gently shaking Danny into consciousness. As the fog in his head cleared, he became aware of the stiffness in his legs and neck. He shook his head to bring himself to full awareness of what was going on.

"Yes, I need to stretch my legs a little bit. Thanks."

After a short respite they were back in the truck and headed north again. "Merci, Max." Danny smiled at the driver. About three hours to go. Danny fell instantly back to sleep.

"Wake up. We're almost there." Danny heard Dimitri's words, but they seemed far away. Danny opened his eyes, looked out and saw the very beginnings of the sunrise. Still dark, but it looked like the night might once again be overtaken by the sun.

"Danny, Max is going to take us all the way to the fish market. There's a lot of fish markets in Paris but he prefers the Poissonnerie Boulonnaise. He can get the best prices there. And besides it's only a couple of blocks from the Left Bank. Maybe we can find a generous soul who will give us a croissant and some coffee. OK with you?"

"Sure, but what's a croissant? I've never heard of that"

"Danny, a croissant is simply a sweet pastry roll. It's shaped something like an Arabic crescent, a cross. Dimitri used his hand to form a half circle to demonstrate. They are a standard for breakfast in France."

"Here we are. Hop out. Merci, mon ami, Max" Dimitri doffed his hat as Max drove away, revealing his shiny bald head. "OK, Danny, let's start walking. Just follow me. Don't look at people and don't bring any attention to yourself. Be sure to keep your hat on. Remember, you are not here legally and you can get into a lot of trouble if you get caught.

As they walked along Danny took in the sights and sounds of

early morning Paris. The shopkeepers opening up their shops and street vendors arranging their wares.

"This is a good place to set up," Dimitri announced. "Look about. There are street vendors everywhere. I feel this is where the tourists will gather. We are on what they call the Left Bank of the Seine River. It is the not-so-expensive part of Paris where many of the famous artists like Picasso, Matisse, and writers such as Hemingway once lived. I think this side is so much more friendly. The other side, the Right Bank, is where the bankers and upper crust people live, along with their expensive restaurants, salons and apartments. We're on the fun side." Dimitri smiled at Danny, making his wide mustache curl up on the ends.

"Look over that way toward the island. Do you see that very large church? That's the Notre Dame Cathedral. It's one of the largest churches in the world. It was built about 800 years ago and took over 200 years to build." Dimitri was satisfied to see Danny nod and the look of awe on the boy's face.

"Millions of people come to see it. They all come along the Left Bank. They are either tourists or on a religious mission of some kind. They bring money and they are ready to spend it. Your job is to give them a few moments pleasure for which many of them will gladly throw some francs into your hat. Here, use my hat. Keep your hat on your head. Sit in that corner and begin playing. Whatever you do, remember you are illegal. I'll be watching out for you. If you hear me whistle grab the money and come towards me, but don't run. I'll figure out which way for us to go."

Danny did as he was told. He sat in the corner Dimitri had indicated, placed his fishing bag behind him so he could comfortably lean up against it and began to play. Since Dimitri had said most of the tourists would be going to the church he decided to play all the church music he knew first. Several of the songs reminded him of the time he had spent with his grandparents and Maggie Ann and he wondered what they would be doing. A few people walked by and a few stopped to listen. One lady even sang along with his music for a few minutes, then she dropped two coins in the hat and moved on. It was a peaceful kind of day and the music brought back so many of his best memories. Danny hardly felt the time passing by.

Hours later Dimitri handed Danny a sandwich and a small plastic cup of wine. "Time for lunch, Danny. Put that money making harmonica aside and get some food in your belly."

"Oh, thank you, Dimitri. Yes, I was getting a little worn out, and I'm starved. I really enjoyed all the clapping and the money people kept throwing in the hat. But my lips are numb and my lungs are just worn out."

"I understand, Danny. You're a fine young man, very caring about others, and hard working, too.

"While you rest let me tell you our schedule. Max delivers twice a week. Tuesday mornings and Friday mornings. That's to meet the largest demands of when people dine out. Of course here in Paris, they are always eating. Today is Tuesday so we have six days until we go back. We can sleep at night in the kitchen of a small bar a friend owns. But we have to be out by daylight. So, over the next several days we can go sightseeing in the morning, before the tourists come out."

"Sounds good to me, I want to see everything we can." Danny replied. "Thank you for the ham and cheese sandwich."

"Well, actually, Danny, here in France we call it a 'croque monsieur'. But you're right, it's just a fancied up ham and cheese.
"Well, I guess it's about time to get back to work. All that money is just walking on past us and staying in the people's pockets. I need to warn you, again, about one thing. If I whistle at you, don't run. Just walk toward me at about the same speed everybody else is. Keep your head down and don't look anybody in the eye. If you run they'll have you. Don't act like you're guilty.

"I'll put the money you've made us in my bag. Don't worry about the money. Half of it is yours, after our expenses. You are doing very well. It's your talent that makes the people so generous." Dimitri emptied the hat and gave it back to Danny who placed it in front of him before he began to play once more.

For the rest of the afternoon coins and paper money steadily flowed into Dimitri's awaiting hat. Danny was exhausted. He hadn't played his harmonica so much in his entire sixteen year old life.

"Danny, think you're about ready to call it a day? It's getting dark and nobody will be out as much after dark, they will be dining or in the bars. Let's go see my bar owner friend."

"Boy, am I ready to quit, Dimitri. We had a good day. As tired as I am, it was still fun." Danny swooped up the hat, once again full of coins and paper money."

The pair began walking down the darkening streets of Paris. The street lights were popping on and the lights of Paris began twinkling across the city and reflecting in the Seine.

"Here we are, Danny. The Gypsy Bar, they call it. It's not really Gypsy, but having us in there helps them show a little Gypsy ambience. The tourists love it. They'll feed us, too. Just be sure to act Gypsy. Americans didn't come all the way here to see more Americans. You might play a little Gypsy music on your harmonica on their small stage to pay for our supper. I'll mention that to my friend to see if he will allow it as a way of saying thanks!" Dimitri grinned again.

"Later tonight, we sack out in the kitchen. Tomorrow, why don't we go see the Statue of Liberty. It's only about two kilometers from here. We can walk it easily, straight down the Seine River. We'll pass the Eiffel Tower on the way."

"But the Statue of Liberty is in New York!"

"Danny, you have a lot to learn. Actually, there are versions of the Statue of Liberty everywhere. I'll tell you more in the morning." Danny's meager bed in the bar's kitchen felt so good after a very long day running from the Gendarmes in Marseille, the long trip north to Paris and then all day playing his harmonica in Paris. He slept very well.

"Bon jour, mon ami, Danny. That's 'good morning, my friend' in French. I figure you need to be learning a little bit of French.

You say it."

"Bon jour," Danny made a stab at it, using his best French accent.

"Very good, mon ami. Grab your bag and let's go. Be sure to keep an eye on it. The biggest business in Paris is pick pocketing. Wherever you see large numbers of tourists there will be pick pockets. And they are very skilled. They will get and spend your money before you even know it is gone. Remember, that is the way they make their living."

"Dimitri, I keep my fishing bag strapped across my body at all times. I am used to the weight of it." Even as he said it Danny pulled the precious bag tighter against his side. The money was one thing, but his Daddy's things were priceless.

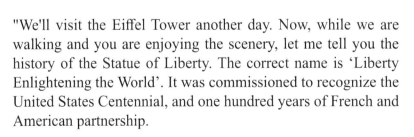

"Here, let's go this way towards Quai de Montebello. Then we'll walk the entire way along the river. You'll first see Notre Dame on the right, then after a few more blocks you'll see the Eiffel Tower on the left.

"We'll visit the Eiffel Tower another day. Now, while we are walking and you are enjoying the scenery, let me tell you the history of the Statue of Liberty. The correct name is 'Liberty Enlightening the World'. It was commissioned to recognize the United States Centennial, and one hundred years of French and American partnership.

The Quest

"In 1886 the statue arrived at what is now known as Ellis Island, to a big celebration. It had taken an extra ten years to get there because of a lot of political indecisiveness. Politicians have always argued with each other just to delay progress.

"In 1889 a thirty-seven foot version of the statue was inaugurated by Americans living in Paris and placed on an island in the middle of the Seine. It has two dates on it, July 4, 1776, for the American Revolution, and July 14, 1889, the French Revolution. The French Revolution is our national Independence Day. That's when we stormed the Bastille, the prison, where they kept all the political prisoners. We call it Bastille Day.

"Look over there at the island. Looks exactly like the one at your American Ellis Island, don't you think? You may have seen pictures of it somewhere. If you've never seen it you now know what it looks like and you even got to see the French one first. So what do you think of Paris so far, mon ami?"

"Dimitri, so many people and they are all going in every direction. Their police cars have funny sirens. I've never seen so many people smoking. Everybody smokes here. Some of the cigarette smoke smells funny, very sweet smelling.

"And those metal circular stands on the sidewalks. They start about knee height and go up just above the head. You walk in it and have a very small amount of privacy. Is it what I think they are? For men?"

"You are exactly right, Danny. We call that a pissoire. We French men feel that when you've got to go you've got to go. Some day those will all be gone. As more and more Americans visit France we're starting to be up tight about doing such stuff in public.

"And all those many people, why don't you listen to them a little bit? You'll hear a lot of different languages. Look at their clothing. Americans have creases in their pants. We don't see any reason. Americans wear white socks. We tend to be a lot more conservative in our clothing. Yes, when you've been here a while you'll be able to look at people and know almost immediately where they are from.

"In your case you blend in pretty good. You're not over dressed and you don't have a short haircut. In fact you almost look like an American 'beatnik'. They dress the same all over the world. So you blend in very good.

"And that funny smelling smoke. Funny thing about that. You see it all the time. When people are visiting a country they feel the local laws don't apply. That's why they often end up in jail. What you smell is probably marijuana. Yes, it's illegal here, but our police and Gendarmes usually ignore it. That's why it's so popular.

"We need to head back now. It's about time for the tourists to finish their late breakfast and start walking the streets looking for a place to put their dollars and francs. You need to be there to help them." Dimitri smiled.

As they walked Danny was aware of the many colorful shops and outdoor cafes. A short time later Danny and Dimitri found a very busy spot. Danny sat and placed Dimitri's hat in front of him, whipped out the harmonica and started playing a lively Gypsy medley by Johannes Brahms, a German composer. The francs started flowing almost immediately. Danny kept his head down as he was instructed. Just smiling and never speaking.

Finally it was time for a sandwich and a small plastic cup of wine. Danny started to stand up when suddenly there was a commotion among the people around him. Danny looked around for Dimitri who signaled him to slowly get up, gather his belongings, and follow him.

"Danny, don't look back. Don't run. Just walk down the street at the same pace as everyone else. You see, when the police are about to make a raid on street vendors like you, they all arrive in a police passenger van. Most of us saw the van coming. So before the police even unloaded everybody was gone. The police will look about and walk around a little bit and then get back in their van and leave. They've done their work for the day.

"We've walked about a block now. Let's stop here for a few minutes. Let's just stand over in a corner. Eat your sandwich and let's see if they come back."

"Dimitri, you've talked about the Gendarme and the police. Are they the same?"

"No, Danny. Police are more local. Gendarmes are a higher level of police. Think of them as being the state police.

"Are you ready to get back to work? Good, I'll stand over here and keep an eye out."

Danny sat down on a ledge at this new spot and reached for his money-making harmonica. Dimitri leaned over to put the collection hat in place when suddenly there was once again a commotion among the people all around. He saw Dimitri falling

forward, and, not knowing what to do, Danny quickly grabbed the hat, his bag and slipped his harmonica into his pocket, moving backward and allowing several people to block him from view. He then turned and began walking away until he could figure out what was going on. When he looked back he saw police chasing Dimitri. A scared Danny continued walking away as fast as he dared, but trying to blend in with everybody else. He had no idea what a French jail would be like. He didn't speak French. He had no passport. He had entered the country illegally and was not even registered at a hotel of any sort. He had to get away.

After walking several blocks along the Seine he found a quiet bench where a few tourists were walking by. "This seems like a safe place," Danny's thoughts raced. "I can see a little way down the street, in case police come my way. I'll just keep my harmonica in my pocket. This evening I'll go back to the Gypsy bar and hope to see Dimitri."

Hours later Danny was getting thirsty. So he went looking for something to drink. Finding a pissoire along the way was a perfect spot to stop for momentary relief. Finally he saw a street vendor selling small plastic glasses of wine. Fortunately Danny still had a little jingle in his pocket. After drinking the wine Danny walked a short distance further, worrying about Dimitri. He had heard a lot of stories about police in other countries. Danny found another bench and rested.

"July, 1959," Danny thinks to himself. "I'm sixteen years old. I've skinned and cooked rattlesnakes, shined shoes, stowed away on a ship carrying kidnapped people and almost got caught myself. I've lived with Gypsies and now here I am in Paris. Seems to me that a person can do just about anything they set their mind to. This isn't really where I want to be in life. But life has certainly been exciting so far.

"Question is where do I go from here and how do I get there. I think when I get back to Marseille I'll try to figure out how to get to Florence, Italy, and then perhaps cross the border into Russia. I'll need some good advice on that part because I hear the Russians shoot people. I also need to go back home some day. But while I'm here I'm going to see and do all I can. For now I'll just sit here and watch the boats go by."

The warm July afternoon and the early hour he had gotten up soon lulled Danny to sleep. He awoke with a jerk. "I must have fallen asleep. I guess I've been here several hours now," Danny said to himself. "The sun is about to set. Summertime sun setting means it's probably around eight o'clock or so. So I'll head to the gypsy bar and look for Dimitri."

After several blocks of walking Danny arrived at the familiar spot and went straight to the owner. "Have you seen Dimitri?"

"No, we haven't. You'd better not play tonight. We hear there were several raids today. The police may have him and they might come here looking for you. Here, have a bowl of soup and eat it in the kitchen. You need to stay out of sight. When we close find yourself a spot on the kitchen floor but you need to leave immediately after we open," the owner said in very accented English. The kitchen floor was hard and dirty, but Danny was grateful for the refuge. He used his cap and vest for a pillow. All night long he barely slept. "What happened to Dimitri? How will he get back to Marseille? Were the police looking for him, too? What was going on?" Danny was fearful for Dimitri and couldn't shut down thoughts of his arrest and even torture. The night slowly drug on until sleep eventually took over.

Before the first rays of daylight Danny was awake and slipping out the door. Outside he looked all about for police and then tried to figure which way to go. Across the street behind a sign he saw the outline of a familiar figure. Dimitri! It was Dimitri!

"What happened?" an excited and relieved Danny asked.

"Danny, yesterday, the police were headed directly your way. So when they got too close I acted like I was stumbling, intentionally stumbling into them, and then I took off running. So they chased me and left you alone. They hauled me off to jail and locked me up overnight.

"This morning, bright and very early, they checked me out and couldn't find anything. I told them I was running because I was scared. Police always grab Gypsies. They don't need a reason. They always think we did it. In this case they had no reason. So

I paid a small fine which probably went into their pockets and they let me go. Have you eaten anything yet?"

"No, I haven't. I'm starving. The more I drink your French coffee the more I like it. The croissants are good too."

"Danny, Why don't we try a different place? There's a big tourist area about 3 or 4 kilometers from here. It's called the Basilica of the Sacré Cœur. What really matters to us is that the Basilica is in the eighteenth arrondissement. You would call it a city district. We've been in the fourth. So it's all different police and Gendarmes who don't know us. If we are seen in the fourth, the Notre Dame area, they'll grab us just for the fun of it."

"Whatever you say."

"Danny, let's stop in here at this photo place and make a photo of you. I have an idea I want to try." Danny indulged Dimitri by having his picture taken. "Today is Thursday, isn't it?" asked Dimitri.

"Yes, it's Thursday. But what are you going to do with my picture?

"You'll see. Tell you what. You just stay right there on that bench and I'll be back soon. Remember, don't talk to anybody. Don't look anybody in the eye. Have a very slow cup of coffee and act like you are just admiring the city."

Danny sat on the bench for what seemed like hours. Finally he got up and slowly walked around while keeping an eye out for Dimitri. He watched a clock on a tower not far away.

"Dimitri, it's been almost three hours now. I've been worried you were picked up again. Where have you been?"

"Danny, do you remember I told you that we Gypsies have contacts everywhere? Many of us have climbed into respectable jobs. But we all remember where we came from. I've been to see a friend in the passport office. This is your French passport," he handed a passport to Danny.

"You are legal now. Well, almost, it won't stand up to a lot of scrutiny, but most people will accept it. Danny, I'm thinking we need to get on back to Marseille. We can catch the shrimp truck tomorrow morning at daylight. Meanwhile, you have made a lot of money both for yourself and for our clan. So why don't we just walk the streets and sightsee? Anywhere you would especially like to go?"

"Dimitri, you amaze me. Don't you ever get tired? Why don't we just slowly head back to the Gypsy bar? Maybe we can sleep there again tonight and make some more money before going to bed. Then early tomorrow morning we can get to the fish market in plenty of time to catch Max before he heads back. Remember, you said he arrives Tuesday Mornings and Friday mornings? We've only been here a couple of days but I've had enough excitement and I'm ready to head back."

That evening in the Gypsy bar, Danny and Dimitri got a very pleasant and unusual treatment. After a good number of people had arrived for dinner and some wine, the owner asked Danny for his fishing bag. Then he pulled Danny up in front of everybody and announces first in French and then in English. "My friends, thank you all for making us your second home. Tonight I would like to introduce a person who's father helped us get our freedom from the hated Nazis. He fought for the United States Army here in France. Then he fought in Korea and there he received a very high medal from President Eisenhower for saving lives. Danny, show them your flag and the medal. As Danny pulled his treasured flag from the bag and shook the wrinkles out best he could, the owner continued, "Sadly, Danny's father was killed in combat while saving the lives of those soldiers. Tomorrow Danny will be leaving Paris, but tonight he is here with us. His daddy taught him how to play the harmonica and tonight he will be playing for us. I beg, encourage, and plead with you to show Danny our French appreciation for his father and for all Americans. Please put tips for him here in this jar and please make those tips very generous."

The rest of the night Danny played and everybody drank more than their share of wine. It was a night to celebrate America and the son of an American soldier who was a true hero.

That night the Gypsy bar stayed open much later than usual and the tips were large. The next morning Danny felt the "morning-after" effects of too much wine. He tried to clear his head as he gathered his few belongings. He managed to remember his fishing bag and re-folded the flag to fit back inside, making sure all the earnings were still there. Slowly, with Dimitri's help, he drug himself to the fish market. Max was there and cheerfully greeted them with his usual "Bon jour, mon ami."

Danny just mumbled, got in the truck, and immediately fell back to sleep. Hours later, they stopped somewhere for coffee.

"Are you feeling better, my friend?" Dimitri asked.

"Dimitri, how do you people stand to drink so much?"

"Danny, we French grew up on wine. We've been drinking it all our lives."

"Well, it tasted good last night. But I sure paid for it this morning. My system will never get used to drinking wine instead of water."

"Danny, you did good last night. We French like to party and you gave everybody a good reason to party. Everybody had a good time. And....we made a lot of money. You did all the work, but I guess I did my part by watching out for you."

The rest of the afternoon Danny started thinking about Buford. "Buford is the reason I wound up in Marseille. I had to do something to get away from him. No telling how he's been treating my mama. And what about my brothers? I bet Buford did something with them. If I hadn't left when I did I might be on some slave ship. I'm going back home and I'm going to teach Buford my name's not 'Boy!' He's not going to get away with any of that 'boy' stuff. I'm not a kid any more. I've learned that I can accomplish anything I want. And what I want now is to teach Buford that he's been messing around with the wrong family. As soon as we get back to Marseille I'm going to figure out how to get back to Chicago."

When they arrived at camp everybody welcomed them. Dominick, the Rom Baro, was especially appreciative that Danny had earned them so much money. He sent someone for wine, whereupon Danny said "No, no, no, no, I'm never going to drink wine again, thank you though."

The Baro gave Danny an understanding smile and said "Sure, son. Now for a nice surprise for you. I have a letter for you from America, and when you get through reading it I have a very special request. It seems the letter was sent simply to "Mr. Danny Carmichael, Gypsy Camp, Marseille, France. Somebody at another camp first received it and knew we had made friends with an American. So they thought it might be for you. First, I couldn't help but see the return address. You didn't tell us Professor Cosmos was a friend of yours. They stayed here with us years ago, and we helped them stow away on a ship to America. They are among the best people we have ever known. Here's the letter."

An excited, but nervous, Danny took the letter from his friend and found a quiet spot to read it.

Dear Danny,

I hope this letter finds you well. We feel you are probably in Marseille now. I hope you've managed to see the Cezanne painting. I just want to update you on your mother and Buford. Right after you left the police raided their apartment but found nobody there. Several neighborhood children were missing. The police felt Buford kidnapped them. They felt Buford was part of some child kidnapping ring where he would abduct them and then sell them to be sent to some of the North African countries to be slaves and Lord only knows what else.

Danny, we think you got out just in time. According to police they were actually kidnapping kids and then selling them to people who would smuggle them on ships.

The police feel Buford and your mother headed back out west somewhere. They also have a report of a stolen truck.

Danny, Karan and I really enjoyed getting to know you. You are an outstanding young man and we care very much for you. We hope you will come our way again. We will always have a place for you in our home.

Much Love
Your friends, Professor Cosmos and Karan,

While reading the letter Danny felt a slow burn and steadily became more and more enraged. After reading the letter again, and then a third time, he became furious. "I'll get him. I know where they went. They are right back there in Arizona. And I now know what he was doing with all those late night trips to Mexico. I'll get the police on him and he will never be able to treat people wrong again."

Chapter 13

Slipping Across the Russian Border

Noticing the boy's growing agitation, the Rom Baro walked to where the trembling Danny now stood. "Danny," the Rom Baro spoke softly, "Go ahead and drink this glass of wine. The wine will help you settle down.

Danny blurted out his plan to go after Buford to his friend who said, "I understand how you feel. You can't do that all by yourself. Let me help you. "I can get you on a ship straight to the United States and you won't have to stow away. I'll help you. I have a plan."

"Dominick," Danny said to the Rom Baro, "Whatever you can do to help I would really be grateful. I need to get there right away, and I need to stop him fast."

"Danny, ships going to the United States dock here regularly. I can get you a job as a deck hand on one of them. You would be fed and you would have a place to sleep, but I need a bit of time to set it up.

"In the meantime, can you do something for us? Danny, this is an enormous favor to ask of anyone and I have no right to ask this of you. You are in no way obligated to do this but I ask it out of desperation. It would mean so much to so many people and save a lot of lives. I would like to ask you to take a message to one of our Romani clans in Russia. This is a very dangerous request; you might even be killed. Danny, I pray you won't come to harm, but the possibility is there and I have to warn you."

Danny sucked in his breath when the Rom Baro spoke about possible death. He had faced death while stowing away on the ship. He had faced it again when he and Alessandro jumped the ship and made it to shore. It sounded like the same all over again.

"We Romani can't do it because we will be spotted immediately. As you already know, we are watched. And we look different. You Americans must eat a lot of sugar. You are all much taller. And you have a lighter complexion."

"I have faith in your cleverness and your ability to make good decisions. You see, the Russians are trying to kill our clans who subsist behind their borders. The Russians have been starving them but that didn't work because our clans have always been able to find food. So now they are holding all the medicines. Our people can't get medicine. They are dying. We have a ship of medicine ready to go to them. The ship will drop anchor far out from shore and the clans must send "fishing boats" to meet it and load up, late at night. But first we must get a message to the clans so they will know when and where to meet the boat."

It will all be in a special code we developed after the war was over. What I'm thinking is you go out with one of the "fishing boats" when they go to take medical supplies off the ship we send. Then you stay on that ship and they will return you to us here in Marseille. Total time about a week. Danny, will you take the message?

"Dominick, if I can help save lives of course I'll do it. That's exactly what my father did. He gave his life to save others. There is something in the Bible about being willing to lay down your life for a friend. Just tell me what to do and get me started on my way." The plan was sealed with a strong handshake.

"I should have arrangements made by the time you get back for your return to the United States. I think the Port of Galveston is in Texas. Maybe I can get you on a ship headed there. Then you would be part way to Arizona, which is where you want to go, isn't it?" Danny confirmed with an affirmative nod.

"The way this would work is, I can get you on a truck headed to Italy. From there you can get to Yugoslavia. That's a country just past Italy on the other side of the Russian border. It's about a two day drive. You can get across the Italian border using your French passport. I'll send Dimitri with you. You two seem to be getting along very well. Dimitri will tell you the rest as you travel."

"I think we need to give you a travel name, one that everybody will immediately recognize. What if we call you The Border Phantom? People might forget your name, but they'll surely remember that.

"The Border Phantom?" Danny grinned at the thought. "That sounds like a super hero from the comic books. I like it!"

"Danny, you know that we are very poor and humble people,

but you will always be one of us," the Rom Baro said. "We will be your family, always. Right now, you must get a good night's sleep. You've had a very long day. I want you to think very hard about what I have asked you to do. We'll talk more in the morning. You are allowed to have second thoughts."

Danny tossed and turned all night worrying about his future. He wanted to get home to help his mama. But he also wanted to help his friends-his new family. The Border Phantom! What a nifty name!

Early the next morning Danny found Dominick, the Rom Baro, was already awake and sipping the hot brew they called coffee. "No second thoughts. l'll do it," said Danny. "Having your help to get home will make it a lot easier on me. And, of course, I want to help the Romani people."

"Excellent," replied the Rom Baro, pounding Danny on the shoulder. "Today I'll send my daughter, Juliette, to take you to the Gulf of Marseille, to the site where Cezanne painted his masterpiece and which you came here to see. You'll like Juliette. She's been at another camp so you haven't met her yet. She's a little older than you so I know there will be no hanky-panky," grinned Dom. "She can tell you a lot more about the Romani and how we live. You'll be back before dark and that's when your ride will be ready. It will take me that long to write and encode the message you need to take to our less fortunate brothers and sisters."

A few minutes later the Rom Baro's beautiful daughter, Juliette, stepped out of her crude shelter.

She displayed a friendly smile and was beautifully dressed in the

rich jewel colors the Romani love. "Hello Danny. Are you ready to go?" Juliette asked in a faint French accent. "My father gave me a little money to use. He said paying for everything was the least he could do for what all you are about to do."

Danny's heart thumped as he stuttered an almost incoherent "Yes, I'm ready."

"Well, come along, then. We'll have a good time today. My father told me to talk about anything you want and to show you what we Romani are like. My family and friends call me Juli. She pronounced it 'you-lee'. So since we are to be friends, please call me Juli too.

"My father asked me to explain some of our customs. I can see you are getting to be the age where you are thinking about girls. So we will talk about girls for sure."

Again Danny stuttered "yes" between the thumps of his heart.

"Well, Danny, we must first talk about how to get to the Gulf of Marseille. We'll walk about two kilometers and then take the bus system. I know all the stops and where to change buses. So just come with me and we'll have a relaxing day together. It will keep your mind off the days ahead."

"Now about girls. The way I see it, we Romani struggle too much to just get by in life to even think about each other. I imagine that's why we young people don't focus too much on the opposite sex. Our parents usually select our future life partner and, then when we are old enough, we marry.

"We do enjoy our friends, though. And I know I'll enjoy the day with you, Danny. Now tell me why you are so interested in art, especially that particular painting, so much so that you would travel half way around the world to see the spot. That is a lot of energy spent just from having seen a painting! You must be a very passionate person, Danny."

"Juli, some friends I worked for in Chicago encouraged me to go to an art museum to look at that painting by Paul Cezanne. They said that they met Gypsies living near Marseille, after World War Two, who helped them get to the United States. And that's why I came to Marseille because of the beauty of that painting. Does that sound crazy? I guess it probably does. I also needed to escape from my mother's crazy boyfriend who saw me as just trouble or a way to make money. Now that seems like such a long time ago."

"Danny, who was your Greek friend? My family has helped many people get to the United States for as long as I can remember. Perhaps it is someone I will know too!"

"His name is Kathigitís Cosmos. Kathigitís means professor. He was a great man and taught me a lot."

"Why Danny, he was one of my father's closest friends. He and my father exchanged promises that they would do anything for each other. My father told me about the letter you received. I am so happy you are here to help Professor Cosmos fulfill that promise."

"Well Juli, maybe you could say Professor Cosmos sent me. Who knows, maybe my coming here is no accident. Maybe I was meant to help Cosmos to keep his promise. It's a big wide and, sometimes, mysterious world. I want to know about your people while I'm here. Your father told me some, but I want to know more. Juli, tell me about your people."

"Sure, Danny. But first, there is our bus stop and the bus is waiting on us. Let's hurry." The two youngsters picked up the pace to a jog with Juli waving and shouting something that Danny assumed must be "wait for us" in French. When they reached the bus door Danny climbed the steps in one stride.

"Whew, we made it," Juli exclaimed a bit breathlessly. "Sit here. I'll tell you more about our people when we get there. It's too noisy to talk on the bus," She shouted over the growling engine. Juli reached for his hand. In response to his quizzical look she said, "Yes, you may hold my hand. It is alright, we are friends. That's what friends do in this part of the world."

As they rode on in silence and changed buses three times, Danny held Juli's hand. "It is such a beautiful day. I love France, I love, Marseille, I love life," Danny thought to himself and smiled at Juli, who returned the charm and displayed her beautiful smile.

Finally the old bus hissed to a stop. "This is where we get off," Juli told him. "Let's walk from here. It's about three kilometers. They walked along the cobble-stone streets, being careful not to stumble. All along the way vendors lined the streets with their farm produce. Finally they reached a spot high up on a hill overlooking the gulf.

When she came to a stop, Juli said, "How about this bistro? France is famous for its outdoor cafes. We call them bistros. We can sit out here, watch the people, listen to all the street sounds, enjoy the

breeze and admire the bay. Would you like a cup of coffee and a croissant? We can eat them very slowly and simply take our time. It's a beautiful day out, don't you think?"

Danny was still so awed that he was ready to say "yes" to anything. The strong aroma of French coffee grabbed Danny's attention away from the powerful beauty of both the gulf and Juliette. Real coffee, no matter how strong would taste great!

"Juli, all these very ancient buildings amaze me. I feel like I'm enjoying this coffee right in the middle of a beautiful book of art. How did all this happen? Where did all this come from? I have so many questions."

"Danny, thank you for wanting to know more about us, who we are, and where we live. Why don't I start by telling you about the politics in Europe. Do you know much about how the country is run?"

"No, I barely know which countries are here. All that I know is what I have learned from Cosmos and your father. Really, I have been on the move so much for the last few years I haven't had time to pay attention to much more than where my next meal was coming from."

"Danny, first let me tell you my father was educated at the University of Marseille. I took some European history and political courses there, myself. My father feels our future is in our hands. It is what we make of it. We don't have to just sit back and accept how and where we live. But first we need to know the history of how we got here. My father says I will be a great leader of the Romani some day."

"Juli, I don't understand why we all can't just get along. I don't understand why there are always some people who want to fight others and take away what is theirs."

"Danny, you are my friend and I don't want to offend you. May I please tell you some history from our European point of view?"

"Juli, I would appreciate you telling me."

"Alright then. During World War Two, just over a decade ago, the Nazis tried to exterminate all Jewish people and also all the Romani. Most people don't know about what he did to the Romani. Even during the Yalta Conference, and later, the United States created a new country for the Jews and did nothing for us. They acted as though we Romani didn't exist."

"What's the Yalta Conference?"

"In February, 1945, just before the War was over, leaders of the main allied powers all met in Yalta, a seaport city in a country called Ukraine. There was Churchill from Great Britain, Stalin from Russia, and Roosevelt from the United States. This meeting was just part of a series of meetings where the "Allies" made plans to end the war and to administer the conquered countries."

"OK, Juli, but what does that have to do with me and us today?"

"Danny, Russia was already the main occupying power in eastern Europe. So the three world leaders agreed for them to administer eastern Europe. The Russians made a lot of promises about democracy and democratic elections. They broke every promise immediately. Many of us felt that Roosevelt was already very sick and weak so he didn't argue strongly enough and chose to take their word. We felt he knew they were not trustworthy, but he was just too ill to argue. He wanted it over with.

"No one among us felt the Russians would keep their word. In no time at all the Russians started being cruel to everybody and especially to the Romani. That's why my father asked you to take a message about medical supplies. Their cruelty has not let up and they will not stop until the Romani people are crushed.

"Danny, the Cold War really began at the Yalta Conference. The Russians started taking everything they could, and the Americans watched it happen. The Americans helped western European countries to rebuild and create great countries. In Eastern Europe the Russians took what had been built and destroyed it. Your president should have let General Patton keep on marching and conquer Russia, also. Not one of us believed Patton was killed in a freak auto accident. We think it was a Russian plot. Why, did you know the Americans are already fighting against a Russian trained army in Vietnam, a country somewhere towards Japan?"

"No Juli, I didn't know that. But what does that have to do with you and me?"

"Danny, We need to tell the story to everybody we can. That's why my father sent me to school. I feel someday you could be a great man in America. You might even be in a position to make changes, save lives, and help us all. There is evil out there and the one force that defeats evil is good.

"Whatever happens, Danny, you will always be my friend. Some day you may be in a position to help. Some day you may come back. When that happens I expect to be right here. I will probably be married and have children. But my family will always be your family. Whatever may happen in the future you will always be able to count on me."

Danny listened intently, taking in the impassioned words of his new friend.

Suddenly Juli said, "Show me the palms of your hands." She grasped his opened hands and placed them on both sides of her face.

"Now, just close your eyes and think for a moment. Right now my face, my body, my whole life is in your hands. Someday your hands may be in a position to help many thousands of people." Juli removed the hands from her face and kissed both palms.

"Juli, thank you for the nice compliments. But I can't understand why you think I may be able to do anything. I'm just a boy. I'm nothing special and I don't know anybody who is."

"Danny, you are much more than a just a boy. You, I, and many others like us are the future of the world. In your case you are not just another person. You started your life with nothing. You faced down oppression at every turn of your life. You would not be defeated. Every time you faced obstacles you found a way to overcome them. You have done more than many, many people your age. You have no fear. You are always ready to help others. You make friends everywhere you go. Dimitri told me about you and how you wanted to learn about France. You wanted me to tell you about European history. You asked my father about Romani history. You are very intelligent and always anxious to learn. Some day you will be in a position to use all that knowledge. And when you are I know you will remember all of us. Yes, Danny, you will be a great man someday."

After a few reflective moments Juli leaned back in her chair, briefly admired the gulf and softly asked, "So, did you enjoy the coffee?"

"Yes, Juli, the coffee was good, but the conversation and what you taught me was even better."

Juli pushed her chair back and said, "We probably need to be headed back. Your truck should be ready by the time we get there." Danny jumped up to help her with her chair.

"Juli, I have traveled thousands of miles to see this beautiful scene. I have come close to being kidnapped and sold to evil people. All this because I saw a painting in Chicago. A beautiful lady at the Chicago art museum taught me how important art is. She said when you can actually see something in your mind that it becomes real. And today when you held my hands to your face and had me close my eyes the struggles of the Romani people became real to me. I don't know that I can ever help the Romani. But I will always remember that very tender moment. Today has been a very special and emotional day to me. Let's turn and look back at the incredibly beautiful Gulf of Marseille one last time while we are standing here."

As they slowly walked the three kilometers back to the bus stop Danny committed to memory every scene, every vendor, every sound. This, today, is why Danny had stowed away on a ship to come to France. Danny wanted to remember everything. Someday, he knew, he would be back.

As they bumped along on the bus and during the bus transfers Danny's mind wandered back to his new assignment, he watched how everyone dressed, how they walked, talked, and gestured with their hands. The next day he would have to blend in. Maybe his life would depend on it. The Border Phantom would have to be hyper aware of everything and everyone around him. He wondered if his father had ever felt this almost unbearable sense of responsibility for the people around him when he was serving in the army. He felt a momentary connection to his father that he had never experienced before. Maybe his dad was watching from heaven right now. Danny hoped so. He also hoped to make his Daddy proud by making a difference in the lives of the Romani.

A short time later they reached the last stop and, glad to depart the bus and stretch, they started walking to the Romani camp where they were greeted by Juliette's father, the Rom Baro.

"Danny, all is ready for your truck ride to where you will cross the border into Russian country. Dimitri will drive you part of the way and will tell you all he can. Again, I will keep your fishing bag for you. If the Russians were to catch you with that they would immediately label you a spy and you would never see daylight again, if you were able to see at all. You are about to head into a very dangerous place." Dom handed him an envelope containing the all important encoded letter. "Guard this well, my son, it will save many Romani lives." Danny placed it securely under his shirt.

The small, wiry, dark skinned man looked Danny in the eye. Danny saw the kindness and the concern in those large dark eyes. The man put his strong arms around Danny and gave him a hug. "I will pray to our God, and all the saints for your safe return. And yes, my daughter will want to hug you also. I know you had a good day together. Danny, you, for the rest of your life, will be part of our family."

"Let's go," interrupted Dimitri. "We need to get on the road. We have a long drive but there is so much to tell you on the way, the time will be filled. The Gypsy clan's old truck blew out a puff of smoke as Dimitri climbed up into the cab and started it."

After another brief hug with the Rom Baro, and a long, very tender hug with Juliette, Danny gave them a final glance and a brief smile. He saw they both had tears in their eyes. Danny climbed up into the passenger's side of the cab and pulled the heavy door closed.

Immediately Dimitri began to explain the journey ahead of them. "We're going to see some beautiful scenery along the way as we drive through the French and then the Italian Riviera. We'll go past Monaco where all the movie stars and the rich people go to play. But let's get out of Marseille first so there won't be so much traffic and we can talk better. It's about 900 kilometers to where we're going, or about 550 miles. Drive time will be about ten hours, although I expect it will take a lot longer than that, because there will be heavy traffic. We will be traveling a major highway."

Dimitri maneuvered the truck through the city of Marseille, saying little while keeping focused on avoiding any traffic mishap that might cause them delay or a brush with the Gendarmes. Finally he broke the silence saying, "Well, Danny, we are about to be out of the city so let me tell you what to expect next."

You already know that you are carrying a secret encoded message that will tell the date, time and exact location for the medicine ship we are sending to our Romani families. The code is used only by Romani. Very few people know about it. But it is written to appear like just another letter, so it won't be an obvious spy letter."

Danny was startled to hear himself called a "spy." He was just a kid, how could he be a spy? He had not considered that this mission could be looked at as such, suddenly the gravity of the situation felt more like a lead weight placed on his shoulders. But he didn't have time to think much about this as Dimitri continued to explain more details about the plans.

"We will drop you near a Romani camp just east of Venice. There, they will give you updated information on how to get through Trieste, Yugoslavia to our oppressed Romani families in Russia. You will take the message to them and then remain with them until they set out to the medicine ship. You will board the medicine ship and they will return you to our Romani camp in Marseille. Our Romani friends in Trieste are already sending out fishing trips every evening to get the Russians used to them going out, and avoid raising their suspicion.

"Now I will tell you about Trieste. It's a major shipping port for much of north and central Europe. When the powers-that-be divided up all the countries after World War Two, they decided to make Trieste what they called an "open city." That means a city where anybody would be able to travel, regardless of nationality. But that has never worked. The Russians took over immediately. Now the border seems to be wherever the Russians want it, and it changes daily, often from street to street. That's why you'll need to talk with local Romani who are staying much more up to date."

"Dimitri, yesterday Juliette told me about the Yalta Conference. Now you are telling me even more. Wasn't the war over fourteen years ago?"

"Yes, Danny the war was over. The Americans had a big parade in Paris and then mostly went home. But many thousands of us are still living the war every day and many of us are dying every day because of the agreements at the end of the war. That's why we are asking you to slip across the border to help our people. You don't look Romani. When our people travel the Russians just grab them and we never see them again. You look like you could probably be European and could at first glance fit in. You might pass the casual observer. But you'll have to be really careful to blend in, just like we talked about in Paris. Remember, your French passport will only pass a very casual observer and you don't speak French.

"When we cross the border into Italy they'll inspect the truck for illegal shipping. They'll also check our passports. Just show your French passport and mumble. They'll be too busy to say or ask much."

"Now just lie back and sleep. We have a lot of time before we get there. And once you get there you may be running so much you'll have no time for rest. Sleep while you can."

A few hours later Dimitri jostled Danny awake. "We're almost at the Italian border," he said. "We're in luck. Like always, traffic is very heavy because this is a major highway for both tourist and commercial traffic. So here's what you do. Act like you are asleep. They will come to the window and I will nudge you and say 'wake up' in French. You act like you just woke up and thumb the passport up. Be sure to let them see your face. They are always looking to see if you have any obvious extreme communicable disease."

In a few minutes the passport control official approached their truck. Dimitri jostled Danny who acted just as he was told. The official waved them on just as they hoped. After several minutes they both let out a big sigh of relief.

"Sure would be good if Trieste were that easy, but don't count on it. If you are able to get past those ever-changing borders, you may officially be called the Border Phantom," Dimitri laughed. "Now go back to sleep. I'll wake you up a couple of hours before we get there and I'll tell you more." Danny was happy to follow that order. The day on the gulf seemed like a lifetime ago already and the seriousness of his mission was adding a heaviness to his heart. He was asleep in a matter of minutes.

"It's time to wake up, sleepy head. We are nearing our point. Sorry you didn't see any of the great scenery today. But we had a good trip. Now it's about to get rough on you. We will be nearing our point shortly where we transfer you over. There it is now. Here, put this purple handkerchief in your pocket with a little bit showing. You will get out and kinda loiter about. Our Romani will contact you. They will know who you are by the color of the handkerchief. They will even call you by your first name. You will go with them and do whatever they say. If the Good Lord is willing, Danny, we'll see you in a few days. God speed!"

"Dimitri, thank you for all your help," Danny gave Dimitri a friendly slap on the arm and exited the truck.

Danny walked away dodging between vehicles at the crowded petroleum refueling station. Momentarily a man bumped against him and then apologized, "So sorry, Danny, you got a light?" The shabbily dressed man held up a cigarette. Danny immediately shook his head, being careful not to talk until it dawned on him this man had called him by name. Again the man asked "You got a light, Danny, or not?" Danny quickly nodded his head. The man said "follow me and get in the truck."

In the truck the shabby dressed, stringy haired man said in very accented English "My name is Lorenzo and our driver is Francesco. He doesn't speak much English, but no problem. We are all very glad to meet you, Danny, and we are all very grateful for all you are doing for us Romani.

"We have a slight plan change. So sit back, enjoy the trip and let me tell you all about it. First, we are not going to Trieste. There's a lot of Russian activity in that area so we are going way north to a small farm house where you and I will spend the night. Then a local boy will help you cross the border early in the morning.

"The problem is that Americans have started coming in. There is a very popular ski resort city just north of Trieste named Udine. We will be going near it on the way to the farm house. The Italian Air Force has an anti-air-craft installation set up there. Well, it looks like the Americans are going to haul in nukes for the Italians to mount to their anti-Russian missiles. So Russians and Americans both are crawling all over the place. You won't recognize any of them because they won't be in uniform. We need to stay far out of their way. Our driver will drop us near the woods where we will get out and walk about five kilometers through the woods to the farm house. The owners are all related to me. So it's safe.

"I will go with you as interpreter. We will spend the night at the farm and then long before the sun comes up you will be on your way through the woods and across the border. My twelve year old nephew will help you get started on the trail. You will start out very early so you can get through before the Russian patrols come along. They are very lazy and do not wake so early. Have you got everything so far?"

"Lorenzo, I am very honored to help out but I still don't understand why I am the only one to do this. You have so many who know all this so much better."

"Oh my young friend, Danny, you do look very different. Here in Europe we can spot foreigners and locals just at a glance. You look very European. Many, perhaps most Russians, also look European. Nobody will give you a second glance.

"Now then, where did I leave off? Oh yes, tomorrow morning Leonardo, my nephew, will take you about three kilometers through the woods where he'll give you more instructions about which direction. Then you'll walk about another two or three kilometers alone, towards a small road. That's about five American miles all together."

"They do have regular patrols, but we pray you are gone long before they arrive. Here is a cheap local watch. You will need to meet a truck before nine o'clock. This truck will take you about two to three hours south where you will get out and then walk through the woods toward a Romani camp."

"But how do I know which truck?"

"Oh, sorry I didn't tell you. It will be an old beat up black truck and the right front fender is red. It will stop beside a tree that is charred from the mid-point up from being struck by lightning. There is a large shoulder in the road there and trucks often stop when they are on long trips. Most places along the road are too narrow to pull over. Two men will get out and head to the tree line to urinate. When they look your way and nod you will quickly look all about to make sure nobody else is anywhere around. Then you will quickly run and crawl under the blankets in the back where you will stay hidden until you stop again and they motion for you to get out. Make sure you wait till they signal you."

"When you do get out, you will be in another forest. You will walk into the woods and straight ahead for about eight kilometers. That's another five American miles. Stay away from all foot patrols. Act very nonchalant if you come across other people. When you see our Romani brothers and sisters you will hand them your letter and then take all instruction from them.

"Ah, here is my family's farm house where we will spend the night." Danny's head was spinning with all of the instructions. How was he going to remember all of this? Could this really work? He gladly climbed out to stretch and take in the charm of the little house with a plume of welcoming smoke rising from the chimney against the twilight sky. At this elevation the evening was cool.

"Just be very polite and sleep where they show you. You will be getting up very early. Remember, we are on the allied side of the Russian line, but the Russians are everywhere and they don't care about what they call "stupid pretend lines." We are dealing with very bad people. My family is risking their lives by participating in this mission as we know you are."

As they stepped to the front porch of the farmhouse, Danny could smell something cooking. Suddenly his stomach rumbled and he remembered he hadn't eaten since the crossant with Juli this morning. A sturdy fair skinned man answered the knock at the door. He greeted Lorenzo with a smile and a clap on the shoulder. The two men turned and looked at Danny,

"Buona sera. Come va? Let's speak English for our young friend, Danny. He will help our Romani families who are suffering under the Russians." Lorenzo said.

"Welcome to our small but loving home. I am Matteo. My wife is Maria and our son is Michele. Michele will take you part way tomorrow morning. Have you eaten? We have a nice pot of soup. And you are welcome to all you want. Maria makes the absolute best soup in Italy."

"Thank you, Matteo, Maria, and Michele. I hope my brief stay here doesn't place a burden on you."

"Danny, we are honored to have you here and we want you to treat us as family. We offer you all of the little that we have. You are helping many of our family members. We will pray for you when you leave us tomorrow morning. Our son, Michele, has been out early many mornings, just hiking through the woods. If any Russians are about they will probably ignore him," the very beautiful and slender Maria said as she smiled at Danny. "Here, you go ahead and eat your soup. I'll fix you a pallet over there in the corner. You'll be getting up very early and there won't be any light to get dressed by. So make sure you know where your shoes and coat are."

"Are you really an American?" asked the excited twelve year old Michele.

"Hush, my son," exclaimed Maria. "Yes, he is. But you need your sleep tonight, too. And you certainly won't be able to talk tomorrow while you're taking him through the woods."

"Danny," Matteo said, "we have very little here but we do have our God. Let's say a prayer for your success. Many lives are depending on you. I'll start it off with the Lord's Prayer, the Padre Nostro, we call it, and then we can have a moment to silently say the prayers in our heart.

"Padre nostro che sei nei cieli,
sia santificato il tuo nome;
venga il tuo regno,

sia fatta la tua volontà,
come in cielo così in terra.
Dacci oggi il nostro pane quotidiano,
rimetti a noi i nostri debiti,
come noi li rimettiamo ai nostri debitori
e non ci indurre in tentazione,
ma liberaci dal male.
come noi perdoniamo chi pecca contro di noi.
e non ci indurre in tentazione, ma liberaci dal male.
Perche tuo e il regno, eil potere e la Gloria,
nei secoli dei secoli.
Amen."

The small Italian family recited it in Italian and Danny recited it in English. Never had Danny felt closer to God. It was with this prayer that Danny once again recognized the gravity of his mission.

"Buona notte, dormi bene," "Good night, sleep well," they all said to each other. Danny retired to his pallet on the floor and Lorenzo found a spot nearby and was snoring softly in what seemed like seconds. Danny on the other hand lay awake staring into the darkness, still feeling the warmth of the soup in his belly. The next day would be very dangerous. Could he possibly do all that was expected of him and not get caught? What would happen to him if he did get caught? Danny shook his head, being sure tomorrow was important, he needed to rest. He recited the Lord's Prayer again partly as a prayer and partly as a way to occupy his mind until sleep could take over.

Try as he might, Danny barely slept. The dangers of the next day kept making their way into his dreams and waking him up.

What if the truck didn't show up? What if the Russians caught him in the woods? What if the Russians had dogs? "My life is out of my control. it's in God's hands." were his last thoughts as he finally drifted to sleep for the last time.

"Buon giorno, Svegliati!" Matteo softly called out.

"Good morning. Get up," Lorenzo translated, even though Danny well understood. Danny pulled on his clothes, then reached for his shoes and his coat. He was grateful that all his clothes, and even his coat and shoes were of European design. The Rom Baro had made sure.

"Are you ready?" asked Michele, as he opened the door to a frigid wind. They were in the Alps and it was alpine weather.

"Danny, I know you can't see a thing. But here's what we do. You walk very close behind me and keep your right hand on my right shoulder. That way you'll know when I turn or when I stop. Being close together will make us look like just one person from a distance. No talking and please walk very quietly. If you want my attention about something just squeeze my shoulder. If you and I are caught they will capture my parents also. My parents are risking their lives to help the Romani, just as you and I are. Where we are now going is very dangerous."

Danny and Michele quietly walked out the door into pitch black wilderness. Michele started a brisk but cautious pace. Shocks of fear alarmed them with every sound of the forest. A startled bird; a rabbit; the wind making eerie moans as it blew through the trees. The swish, swish of their feet as they walked through the leaves sounded like thunder as they tried to avoid every noise. Danny had never in his entire life felt this scared. Michele stopped every few minutes to listen for sounds that didn't belong.

After a short time Michele stopped and whispered to Danny "I can't take you any farther. You keep in the same direction for about two kilometers. That's about a mile for Americans. It is almost daylight so you can find your way ahead. But you will have to be even more careful. I wouldn't expect any Russians out this early or in this area. But you never know. If you do see anyone start picking up sticks like you are gathering firewood then continue gathering and move away from them. Be very careful and try to go as straight as possible so you will come out very near the Lightning Tree. Oh, I want you to visit us again someday, during peacetime."

"I sure will, Michele. Thank you and God bless you and your family," as they hugged, then departed, each going his own way.

Danny was on his own now. Only about a mile to go, or two kilometers as they would say in Europe. Danny watched every tree to see if anything moved. Then he started making his way, very slowly, from tree to tree. At each tree he would pause, look about, and listen. With this cautious approach he steadily moved forward to the road. Then, as he was watching he saw movement behind two trees. They were still a good distance away, so Danny didn't think he had been seen. As he watched he saw the two men steadily moving away. Were they Russian soldiers? Danny wondered. Were they simply hunting for a rabbit for breakfast. No idea. But this made Danny even more watchful.

The silence was broken by the sounds of a big truck on a highway, somewhere straight ahead. Danny started feeling a little easier, knowing he was headed in the right direction. But he reminded himself to be even more cautious. Almost there now. Finally he saw the road. It was a small two lane road without much traffic, it seemed.

Danny found a hiding spot in a small cluster of trees where he could see out easily. Just a few feet and to his left he spotted the Lightning Tree. It must have been an enormous tree before Mother Nature humbled it! The sun had just started between the trees. "In a few minutes it will be warmer," Danny quietly said to himself.

Then he heard the rumble of a large truck. He could see it approaching from a distance. It stopped directly in front of Danny's hiding place. A bunch of Russian soldiers got out of the back and all started towards the trees carrying their weapons. Danny made himself as small as possible and froze, being afraid to even breathe. As he remained so quiet Danny finally realized the Russians were not there for him. There were simply doing what all soldiers do when they see a bunch of trees on a deserted highway. Finally somebody blew a whistle and they all ran back to the truck.

Danny blew out the breath he had been holding. Still safe. They had walked right past him! Another few minutes, then another truck. Danny looked for the fender. Nope. Still not his truck. Then another truck. Red fender. Danny stilled himself awaiting the right signals and hoping no other vehicles came past. The driver parked near the trees so Danny wouldn't have far to run. After a short wait, two men got out of the truck and started towards the tree line. Danny slowly made himself visible. One of the men looked his way and nodded. Danny took off running lickety-split as they would say in Rattlesnake Cove, Alabama. Get under those blankets in the back and hide, the directions ran through his brain. Under the covers he found some food and a canteen of water. "Oh, blessed relief," he said to himself. "I've had nothing to eat or drink all morning." The blankets felt so good. He had been freezing for hours. Now only two or three more hours and he would get out once more, to go and find the Romani camp.

During that travel time Danny fought hard to resist the urge to look out from the covers. With time on his hands and nothing to do Danny started reflecting on what led him to this place and the dangers all around him. This was not his fight. He had no reason to be in Russia surrounded by bad people who would take his life without even a second thought. He might be murdered on the spot. He probably would be beaten. There was nothing good here.

After a long time, Danny's usually ever present positive attitude took over and he began reflecting on the many friends he had made. There was Maggie Ann in Rattlesnake Cove. "I will go back there some day. I hope Grandpa is doing OK. I wonder if the law ever caught her brother for running shine. Danny's jumbled thoughts went to Buford, the most despicable person of all time. The man with a black heart. I will go there just as quick as I can get to the United States. Now I realize what he has been doing. He was kidnapping people and selling them across the border. I'll take care of him and then I'll get the law on him so that he will never see daylight again. I hope my mother is OK.

"It really felt good saying the Lord's Prayer last night with my new Italian friends. I've never known very much about religion before. When I get back to Rattlesnake Cove I need to talk with Maggie Ann's father."

Chapter 14

Gypsy Camp Behind the Russian Iron Border

The sounds of traffic on a busy highway and the jolting of the truck as it bounced over bad roads would not allow Danny to sleep, so he lay still and listened. The sounds of trucks and cars rumbling by faded and then stopped, only the bouncing continued. They must be somewhere on a country road.

Danny felt the truck slow down and then stop. He waited for what seemed like a long time before he heard the truck door open and the sounds of somebody climbing into the back of the truck. The covers were slowly peeled off him. He closed his eyes hoping he would be looking into a friendly face when he opened them. Slowly he opened his eyes and relief flooded over him as he peered into the smiling face of one of the two men who had picked him up hours ago. The man pointed to the forest line nearest the truck and said "dritto, tre kilometri" as he held up three fingers and gestured straight ahead into the woods. Danny had been around long enough now to understand the man probably meant direct or straight ahead and three kilometers. He then made gestures warning Danny to be careful. The man patted Danny on the shoulder and ushered him toward the woods.

Danny was off into the forest. He knew to be very nonchalant and act as if he belonged if he encountered people, but when nobody was around he would skedaddle, as he ran from tree to tree. Then, sensing people about he would casually, but purposefully, walk toward his goal. After a while he smelled food cooking. Somebody nearby was cooking, and those good smells reminded Danny how hungry he was.

What seemed only a short while after beginning his trek into the woods, two men approached him. Their clothes were tattered and they looked scraggly as if they were street people in Chicago, but they acted friendly. Danny thought to himself, "If they are Russian soldiers they would most likely be in uniform. Maybe I have found the Romani already. I may be getting in a lot more trouble here, but I'm going to follow them. Maybe they will feed me." The men motioned for Danny to come with them. Another few minutes through the woods and they arrived at a camp site. All Danny's senses were alerted. He could even smell the salt water of the ocean. But Danny's biggest interest now was food.

They led him to a tree stump and motioned him to sit. Another Gypsy brought him some soup which he drank eagerly. The entire camp of people gathered around to look at this strange new comer. Danny stopped to smile but kept gulping down the soup which was surprisingly good.

After a few minutes a girl about his own age approached him and began talking in fairly good English. "Hello, I am Sofia. I bet you are Danny, The Border Phantom. We knew you were coming, but we did not know when. We have had people out watching for you for days. We began to be afraid the Russians had found you.

The Russians know we are here but they leave us alone because they think they might get sick and we are all dying off anyway. Some of our people are very sick and the Russians won't let us have medicine. They think that is how they will kill us all. And the world will not know about it.

"For now you just sit and relax. You must have been though a lot the last few days. My father will be here soon and you can give him the letter. I know you are curious about me. I have lived through war and hunger all my life. Mussolini, Hitler, and now the Russians. I learned English from some church people. They told me that someday this would be over and the Americans would take care of us. I haven't seen it yet. But we all pray to God that maybe you are the first of many Americans that do care about our people. Danny, that you have risked your life to help us shows that you are a bright and shining light. You bring our people hope."

"Sofia, I am just a guy who got caught up in all this. I am nobody special."

"Danny, you are so much more than that. Here, in our camp, we Romani are very close to God because faith is all we have. We never question how or why God does something. We simply say thank you when we pray. Oh. Here is my father now. I will translate for you."

A big, barrel-chested man with an ear-to-ear smile walked up and stuck out his hand "Gabriele," he said.

Sofia translated as her father spoke. "Danny, we are so happy and grateful you are here. We have been so worried. The Russians are always looking for foreigners. They would have called you a spy and locked you away the rest of your life. Did you bring the letter?"

Danny reached through his jacket and under his shirt where the letter was safely hidden. He pressed out the wrinkles and handed over the letter, then sat quietly while Gabriele studied the code it contained. Finally Gabriele folded the letter and placed it in a pocket.

Once again Sofia translated. "Danny, the medicine boat will be here tomorrow night. With this letter we know exactly where and when. Our fishing boat people are expert navigators and will be able to find it easily. We will hide you here until tomorrow night. When the boats go out you will be with them and then you will transfer to the medicine boat and return to Marseille. I will leave you with Sofia while I go to inform our boat captains and get them ready. She has a lot of questions about America for you."

"Danny, I am very glad to spend some time with you. We all want to know about America. Can you please tell me?"

"Sofia, all I know is what I've done and what I've seen. America is such a big country with so many different kinds of people. We are not all alike. We don't all agree, but most of us love our country. In America there are big cities and small towns. There are rivers and mountains and deserts and forests. It is beautiful, what I have seen of it anyway. Someday I will see it all.

"We are a county of laws and we understand right and wrong. Most of us will try to help those who have been wronged, whether they are in our country or somewhere far away. That's why my father came to Europe to fight in World War Two. That's also why he went to Korea to fight.

"He was killed in Korea and his body was never brought home. There was a big memorial service for him. That's when all my troubles started. I'm sorry, enough of me. I want to hear about you and the Romani. Why do the Russians want to get rid of you?"

"It didn't start with the Russians. Everybody knows about the Jews. At least they had a homeland once upon a time. But we never did. The Romani troubles started in northern India. In India they had what is called a caste system. There you were born into a certain social level of the caste system and that would never change. No one ever had hope of a better life. Why, they even called many people unclean, as though they were garbage. Slowly, but steadily, our ancestors started moving to Europe to get away from it. Because of our dark complexion and black eyes and hair, many people felt we were from Egypt so they called us Gypsies. Wherever we went we were always the outsiders because of our color, and because we clung to our strong family culture. Outsiders are always outcasts when there's a fight for resources.

"Now the Jews have their own country but we have camps at the edge of town. It's just not right. We are good people. And now, you, Danny have risked your life to come help us. "You know what I think? I think all Americans want to help people. I think they will risk their lives to help. You certainly have, Danny. Your father gave his life, too. I think that's why Americans are respected around the world.

"Danny, I have heard that wherever you go you want to help, and you always want to do what is right. And now you have earned the brave name people are calling you, "The Border Phantom."

"Danny, I think if all Americans are like you America must truly be a great country. People talk about America all around the world. And now, after meeting you, I see why. I think, Danny, that someday you will be back and you will be able to do a lot more, even, than you do now.

"Remember this, always, when you come back, and you surely will, look for the Romani people. We have connections all across Europe. We will help you in whatever you are doing, because I know you will come back to help people.

"That's enough talk for now. Let me show you to a hiding place we have prepared for you. Sofia led Danny to a lean-to hidden under some brush. There was a blanket on the ground. It looked very comfortable, but Danny knew better. He had slept on the ground many times and it was never comfortable, but he was tired and grateful.

"Danny, have you rested?" came a soft gentle voice from the edge of his lean-to. Can I get you anything else to eat or to drink?

"Sofia, I must have slept hours. I had no idea I was so tired. Is it almost night time already?"

"Yes, it is. I hope you rested well.

"We have some fresh soup on to honor you." In the old days we would have had a party with lots of music, singing, and dancing. But now we have to be careful to not make too much noise. We don't want to alert the Russians. Some of our people want to thank you for helping us. Some will shake your hand, others will hug you. A few young ones will even curtsy to you, in the old way. They will all try to say thank you in English. Whatever you do be sure to stand and give each one your attention. We all believe very strongly in manners.

"Shortly after we eat everybody will go to bed. That's all we can do without electricity. I'll show you back to your lean-to and then tomorrow morning we'll have some Romani coffee for you."

A woman dressed in once colorful clothes, now faded and ragged, brought Danny a bowl of thin soup. Danny smiled his thank you. Again, he was so hungry that it tasted delicious. He could see the people gathering around to speak to him. Politely, they waited for him to finish his soup.

Each person came to Danny and held out a hand which Danny grasped warmly. A few said thank you in English. Two of the older men gave him a bear hug. The camp was much bigger than Danny had realized. Danny worried about the Russians even though Sofia had assured him no one would talk. If anyone had breathed a word within earshot of the Russians, the whole plan would be over and these good people might be killed. He might be killed.

Finally the only light left was the small camp fire. True to her word Sofia appeared and led him back to his hidden lean-to. Somebody had lit a small candle for him and placed a mug of water.

"I'll see you in the morning," Sofia whispers to him, as if there was not another person in their small world.

Another night. Another hard bed in some remote, strange place. "Probably long and sleepless," Danny said to himself. "Everywhere I've been people have treated me so good, but I would love to be home where I belong. Come to think of it, I haven't had a home since my father died." When he thought of home, he thought of Rattlesnake Cove, church on Sunday, afternoons with Maggie Ann, and helping Grandpa with the animals. That was home. After a few minutes Danny feel asleep. In spite of his long nap, it had been a very long day.

"Good morning, Border Phantom," Sofia's beautiful voice called

out. "I brought you some of our special coffee. Are you dressed decent?"

"Sure, I'll be right out."

"Danny, we all hope to make this a very special day for you. Here, drink your coffee. I know it tastes awful, but it's hot and the best we can do."

"Thank you, Sofia. I got used to coffee made with roasted grape seed back in the camp in France. This will be fine."

"The fishing boat captains are getting ready tonight. You'll go out with them after dark. I'll take you to meet them later on today. But in the meantime I'm going to take you on a little sightseeing and tell you about us. No, we're not going into the city of Koper itself, but I will take you high on a hill where we can look out over the city and also the Gulf of Trieste. From there we can see out to the Adriatic Sea. If we could see far enough we would be able to look all the way across to Venice. We'll take some food and some water with us. Are you ready for a little hike?"

"Oh yes, I am ready. I was cramped up in the truck and then slept and sat around your camp yesterday. I'm ready for some exercise and a hike and some sight-seeing will be good."

"Well, come on then. It's about three kilometers. I'll tell you more as we walk. First, I know you are concerned about the Russians. We all are. They don't all wear uniforms, so no eye contact with anyone. The locals don't want us here either.

"If anybody sees us and you feel you must speak simply say buon giorno. That's 'good day' in Italian. You've probably already heard it several times. Most people around here also speak Italian. And you look like you could be from almost anywhere in

Europe. So we'll do fine."

"Sofia, I just don't understand. Why does everybody want to get rid of your people? You aren't hurting anybody. You're not even living in the best of places."

"Danny, we look different. It doesn't take much for people to want to push others out. There's only so many jobs to go around. There's only so much food.

"People worry about us. They are afraid we will steal their jobs, their money, whatever they have. And to be very honest some of our younger people get frustrated trying to get jobs, so they take what they need. As time goes on I am really worried about the future of our people. I feel things will get worse and worse. Slowly a few of our people are trying to blend in with others. But it's very slow. This problem is why my father wanted me to learn English."

As they walked they had been steadily climbing upward and Danny was beginning to get winded. At last Sofia announced, "Here we are! From this hilltop you can look in every direction and see beauty."

"Yes, that is a pretty view, but not as pretty as you, Sofia," Danny smiled.

"Oh no, Danny," as Sofia pleasantly laughed and stepped back a little. "I have been promised for years and you are leaving tonight. However, you are a very handsome young man and if circumstances were different, who knows?

"What I would like to do, and the reason I brought you up here today, is to show you how much our entire nation needs America. You are the only American I know. In fact, I may never meet another American. We are all good people and we are being treated very wrong. We need help and have no way to get it. We need you to go back to your world and spread the word about the Romani and about all of Eastern Europe. Some day we pray America will intervene for us. We cannot do it by ourselves.

"Look in that direction over the bay. See all the ships coming and going. A ship can load up here and travel all the way south around Italy and then out to the Atlantic. You can go anywhere in the world from here. In fact, all of southern Europe brings their produce here. This entire bay is the main port for all of southern Europe. All food, everything, coming and going comes through here."

"Tell me about the city I see when I look off to my right."

"That is Koper. It was a major city all the way back in Roman times. Beautiful century old buildings. The country we are in is Slovenia, or used to be. It seems like every few years another country has taken over the government and calls it by another name. In fact after World War Two they said we are part of Yugoslavia. I think officially they call us part of the Free City of Trieste, an open port city. Whatever the case we are a beautiful country with thousands of years of history.

"This is a perfect place for us to eat our lunch. All I could find was this small loaf of Italian bread. We don't have anything to spread over it, but I do have a little flask of water. Let's eat and just sit here and admire the scenery." She tore off a chunk from the loaf and handed it to Danny."

Sounds of ships engines and horns drifted up to the hill top from the port below. The breeze picked up and the clouds began to gather and grow dark.

"We probably need to head back, Danny. You need to meet the boat captains and crews. Careful, don't stumble over that rock." Noting that Danny was watching her, as she walked ahead of him, she gently chided him, " You're as silly as a goose. What are you looking at, anyway? You need to watch where you are going!"

After a short time later and more gentle teasing from Sofia they arrived back at the camp.

"I'll take you to my father, then soon he will take you to meet our fishermen.

"Father, here he is. We had a good hike and I think Danny understands us better now. Whatever the case, I feel Danny will always be our friend.

"Danny, I pray you return some day. If you should return, just ask around. I'm sure you will be able to find me. You have inspired me to do all I can to help our people. It is easy to lose hope and, therefore, the will to keep trying, but If you can come all this far to help, then surely I can find a way to do more.

Let me give you a big hug and say thank you for what you are doing." Sofia wrapped her arms around Danny's waist. It was a sweet hug between the new friends. "I'll go along to translate," said the pretty Romani girl.

Sofia translated as Gabriel spoke. "Come with me, Danny. I'll take you down to the boats. They're getting ready now."

After a short hike through the woods and down a boulder strewn pathway, they arrived at the water's edge.

"Danny, this is Simone. He's the captain of the three fishing boats that are going out. He doesn't speak English so you'll just have to trust him and use hand gestures. They know exactly where to go and what time to be there. They will be going out into the international zone. So you shouldn't have any trouble. But remember, the Russians don't play by rules. He'll be leaving at dusk and then running without lights so they can't be so easily seen. Very dangerous to do so, but much safer than alerting the Russians." Sofia translated as her father continued.

"You will be going back to Marseille on the medicine boat. The captain will be expecting you. God speed to you, and we all  thank you and wish you well. Now, I know you hugged my daughter, but I want to give you a man's hug from our entire camp."

As the fishing boat captain began to speak, Sofia translated. "Danny, I am Simone and I am very proud to have you aboard. Just stay down out of the way And I'll get you safely there. I'll get you a heavier coat. It gets cold out on the water. Now please come aboard. I'll show you a good place to sit."

Danny jumped aboard then turned to wave to his Romani friends. The adventure was about to continue. It seemed nobody spoke English so all Danny could do was watch and keep out of the way. A sinewy old fisherman brought him a mug of what seemed to be thin soup. It was warm and felt good going down since he was cold, even with the heavy coat he had been given.

Occasionally Danny saw lights in the distance but none of the vessels approached them. Slowly but steadily they made their way forward. The captain changed course slightly a couple of times, but returned to the same direction. Danny figured this was to throw off anybody who might be tracking them. After what seemed forever they sighted a larger ship in the distance. The ship blinked its lights three times. The fishing boat captain blinked the boat lights twice. Danny felt this must be some sort of preplanned recognition and authentication signal. The boats slowly but steadily, drew near the ship. After a round of shouted exchanges between the captains everything seemed safe. The ship cast ropes down to the fishing boats and the vessels were roped together while the transfer of the precious medicine began.

A couple of sailors helped Danny climb over to the medicine ship. A big booming voice welcomed Danny. "Hello, Border Phantom. I'm Captain Joe. We are very proud to have you aboard. Perhaps you would rather I call you Danny?"

A young sailor handed Danny a mug of real coffee. The first he had in days. Everything would be all right. "Yes, Sir. Danny is just fine. Thank you for helping my friends."

Chapter 15

Back to Marseille and America

P lease come below to my little office, where I run this ship. My people will do all the unloading while we are here. The fishing boat captain will join us for a few minutes. He and I have some coordinating to do."

The two captains drank their coffee and spoke in Italian for a few minutes and then reviewed their maps. Both made pencil notes. It was an excited and active conversation with both captains talking and questioning at the same time. Finally, they seemed to have an agreement, and they both pointed at locations on the map and also made notes in their calendars. The ship captain brought out a bottle of wine and poured glasses of it. The captains toasted each other. A great decision had been made. They shook hands and the fishing boat captain started up the narrow stairs, leaving an intrigued Danny below deck.

Captain Joe turned back to say, "Danny, I must supervise the casting off of lines and then we'll be on our way. I'll tell you everything then." Simone smiled and waved good bye as he prepared to go to his fishing boat.

The lines were all cast off. All three fishing boats were full of medicine. Everybody waved farewell. They were all excited about their success. A lot of people would benefit from this night's work.

When Captain Joe returned to the office he found Danny patiently waiting. "Danny, how about some more coffee. In my many years working with sailors I've learned to always have plenty of coffee available." He set a fresh pot on a little hot plate across the room.

"While that brews let me tell you that we are in international waters now. We are traveling under an Italian trader's flag. The Russians are supposed to leave us alone here, but I don't trust them. They are stealthy and evil.

"Captain Joe, I have to ask, why are you able to speak English so well?"

"Here in this part of Europe we all speak several languages. Most of us speak English because it seems to be the one language that everybody has in common with each other. And most of the schools in Europe teach it because it is an international trade language.

"Let's talk about where we are going and how we will get there." "We are sailing in a south westerly direction. We will be following the eastern coast of Italy all the way down to the toe of the boot. Here, I'll show you on a map. The captain stood over his desk and motioned for Danny to come look, as he unfolded a map. "You can see that Italy looks like a boot. Then we'll start back north on the western coast towards Marseille, France. You will be able to see the coastline most of the way. I expect our sailing time will be about three days total. However, I have a surprise for you When we take this route we always stop overnight for supplies and fuel at my hometown of Villa San Giovanni. Some of my men live there also." He winked at Danny.

"I have already radioed my wife. My entire family will turn out. We'll have a great time. You can stay in my home. My wife makes the best pasta you have ever eaten. We'll have a feast tonight. The priest will be there to bless the food. The mayor will be there and everybody will want to talk to you. Nobody there has ever met an American.

"As soon as we get there you'll have a good hot bath and, later, after the feast, a nice comfortable bed. When's the last time you had a good bath?" Danny knew he was filthy and was embarrassed but Captain Joe gave him a playful push on his shoulder and laughed. "We are sailors, Danny, not gentlemen, few of us notice the smell of a man over the smell of the fish!" Joe laughed another hearty laugh.

Danny tried to smooth out the wrinkles in his well worn shirt and spoke up, "Captain Joe, why all this big party for me?"

"First, let me explain that nobody knows the details of our trip or what you have done. They just know an American is with us and that you have given great help to some of friends in Eastern Europe. We have to keep the details secret or else the Russians might learn and destroy the entire plan.

"Let me tell you what you have just done. Because you delivered that letter, the fishing boat captain and I have set up an international medicine smuggling network. Here's the way it works; I make several port calls starting in Marseille. They are all for the purpose of collecting medicine and medical supplies. Some of my expenses to deliver the medicine will be paid.

"The fishing boat captain and I worked out a plan so he will know my next arrival and the exact location. They will get the medicine and transport it to all the Romani camps behind the Russian border. Danny, we will save a lot of lives."

"All right, I understand. But why you and why are all these people helping? Are they related or something?"

"No, Danny. The people providing the medicine don't know any of the people receiving it. It's just that when people are being evil, good people must step up. And that's what we are doing. You helped make that happen. And besides that, I feel I owe the Romani a personal debt. They saved the lives of my men and me back during the war. We were caught behind enemy lines and they helped us escape. So I am very happy to help them. I feel good people must help each other.

"Now I need to go up on deck and make sure everything is in order. Drink your coffee. The head, what you would call the water closet or bathroom, is in that direction."

Danny leaned back in his seat and slowly sipped the coffee. "Was it all finally over? Could he focus on finding Buford and his mother? Would they be living in the desert again or conning people out of rent money somewhere in Tucson? Whatever Buford was doing Danny knew it would be criminal."

"Danny, come on up on deck and join me. Let's enjoy the ocean air," Captain Joe called.

"Captain, I apologize for so many questions. But this is all so new to me."

"The jovial captain laughed and replied "Go ahead, what's your next question?"

"Well, I feel so stupid asking it but there's no road signs in the ocean. How do you know where you are going?"

"Danny, I do it the same way mariners have done for thousands of years. I use the stars. Even in our Bible the wise men used the stars to find Baby Jesus. Celestial navigation is a science in itself. But once you know how, you can find where you are anywhere on earth. Oceans, deserts, and even in forests. To make it very basic, though, you draw a line from a star, any specific star, to a point on your map. Then you draw a line from another star to your map and where the two lines intersect is your location. Mariners have known for thousands of years the exact location of stars and how far above the horizon they appear from specific locations. You just consult your records and that is it. Well, like I said, pretty basic."

Danny puzzled over what he was told, but he would get the captain to show him on the map later on.

"We should have smooth sailing from here on. You have earned it. We have almost all day to travel. We usually sail in the daytime only and then along the coast. We pull into the ports at night. You'll see a lot of beautiful scenery along the way. The Mediterranean can get rough at times, so be prepared. Are you ready for some sleep? Danny nodded. He was weary to the bone and it showed. "I'll get one of the men to show you to a bunk. You go sleep for a while."

Danny had no problem falling asleep that night. It seemed like he had traveled around the world just to deliver a message. He realized he had a lot more to learn about the world. The ship gently rocked him to sleep.

The sun's bright rays and its warmth woke Danny. He turned

over and looked out. They had traveled from frigid temperatures to perfect summer weather. Coffee would be on and hopefully there would be food. He jumped up and climbed the short flight of steps. Captain Joe greeted him with the same booming voice. "How did you sleep, Border Phantom?"

"Oh, I slept so good, I feel great today. The sun is shining and look at that water sparkle out there!"

"Oh yes, Danny, that's our Italian sun. If you feel good now just wait till tonight. I'll get my son, Adamo, to show you around this evening. He'll make sure you have a good time and see you don't drink too much wine. He's seventeen years old. I think that's about your age.

"What about some breakfast? I'll get Cookie to bring you some. Yes, I've learned over the years the two most important people on a ship are the navigator and the cook. He cooks up a great meal. I think he'll bring you some eggs and sausage, with some cheese on the side. So get ready for a good meal. Eat all you want. I'll leave you alone now. Just enjoy your breakfast."

The day wore on slowly. The breeze was up, but the sea was only a bit choppy. The sun shone warmly the Italian coast as they sailed along. A deck hand brought Danny some oil to spread on himself for protection from the sun. "I could live like this," Danny thought.

Late afternoon Danny could feel the ship turning west. And then later it turned north. Captain Joe came to explain to Danny, "Look off to your right and you will see the very toe of the Italian boot, just like you saw it on the map. We are turning now to go around it and then through the strait that separates Italy from Sicily. They named this body of water the Strait of Messina. The wa-

ters are often very rough because they seem to run in every direction. But I have been through this strait many times over the years. Shortly I will have to call the passage operator to tell him we are coming through. Immediately after we get through you will start to see my little village in the hills to the right. Soon we'll pull into port for an exciting evening."

Danny held on as the tumultuous currents rocked the ship about. After a few minutes the ride became smooth again. Danny could start making out the houses up in the hills.

"Danny," Captain Joe exclaimed. "Look at all those people coming down to the dock to meet us. They always gather to meet their men coming home. On this trip they know we have an American with us. They don't know why we have an American and they also know to not ask too many questions. So there's a lot of excitement in the air, even though they're not sure of the real reason. See the house up the hill with all the grape vines behind it? That's my home. They've got tables set out everywhere and many are laden with food. We are going to have a feast! How much can you eat?"

"Sir, I'm a growing boy and I stay hungry all the time, but that is just too much trouble for me."

Captain Joe cut Danny short, "Danny, this is a big day for them, our ship is coming home and they get to meet an American. There, I see my son, Adamo. He speaks good English also. Just remember, we are leaving tomorrow morning at sunup. We still have a long way to go.

"The first mate will see to getting the ship tied up and secured. As soon as he secures it, we'll get off. Why don't we go straight to my home and get you cleaned up a little bit so you'll be feeling more festive?"

The small crowd started cheering and applauding as Danny came ashore. They felt Danny was somebody special to visit their small village. Everybody wanted to touch him and pat him on the back as they followed along while Captain Joe led him to his home. There were so many people and so much noise that Captain Joe had to tell everybody to wait a few minutes to start the party.

Standing in the door was an attractive lady, Captain Joe's wife, who hugged and kissed her husband and then greeted Danny with a hug and held out some clothes. "She's handing you some of Adamo's clothes to wear. You are about the same size," Captain Joe said. "Take your time in the tub. There's no hurry."

A large galvanized tub filled with good hot water was waiting for him. How long had it been since Danny had been clean? He just couldn't remember the last time he'd had this luxury. He decided he would never take a good bath for granted again. It would be an absolutely great evening.

"Wash my hair, scrub my feet, knees and elbows. Soap up all over. Danny's thoughts happily rambled as he bathed. "It will be a great evening." Danny began whistling "O Sole Mio," the only Italian tune he knew. After a short time he jumped out and dried off. "Clean clothes. I feel good, and I hear music outside."

Danny started toward the sound of music when he saw Captain Joe. "I've got some good news for you, Danny." I just now got a radio message that your friends in Marseille have secured you passage on a ship headed for Galveston, Texas. You will be a cabin boy, paid a salary, and be treated just like any other crew member. Also, the captain of that ship has trucking friends in Galveston. He thinks that one of them may be willing to take you to Tucson. There is one catch though. I need to get you there by tomorrow night. I think I can do that if there are no storms or other problems."

"But, Captain Joe, I need to get my bag and money from my Romani friends and tell them good bye."

"No problem at all, Danny. We'll get into port late tomorrow night and your friends will be there waiting for you. They want to thank you and say good bye. I was told they will bring your belongings. You will need to board the ship immediately because it will depart very early the next morning. What this means is we leave by sunrise in the morning and I will try my best to get you there to meet the ship.

"For now, this night, you must enjoy yourself. Now, I know you will be drinking a little wine. Let me warn you in the very strongest words. Don't drink too much! You'll pay for it tomorrow. Stay with my son, Adamo. He'll take care of you. Now, let's join the party."

As they walked out the door the sizable number of family and friends all applauded Danny. A loud deep voice commanded everybody's attention. "Friends, family, citizens of Villa San

Giovanni, please give me your attention! As mayor of our beautiful villa I would like to say a few things. First, out of courtesy to our guest, I'll speak in English since most of us understand it. We are here this evening to honor a young man for his extraordinary courage. Because of Danny Carmichael, 'The Border Phantom,' an entire network has been set up to help many people behind the hated Russian Iron Curtain. I can't tell you more than that.

"We, here in Southern Italy, do not like to see people mistreated. We know the difference between right and wrong. And we applaud the people who help make things right. I would like to make Danny an honorary citizen of our villa. Does everyone here agree?"

Cheers and applause went out from everybody. It was a unanimous decision. "Thank you. I knew you all would agree. Danny Carmichael, On behalf of and at the request of our beautiful Villa San Giovanni, I proclaim you to be an honorary citizen. If you return in the future you will be always be one of us.

"Father Angelo, will you please bless the food?" the mayor requested." The villa priest blessed the food, speaking in Italian. Danny heard his name mentioned in the prayer, though he could understand little else.

"Now," the mayor proclaimed, "Everybody, fill your glasses and lift them in a toast."

"To Danny," Everybody shouted and glasses clinked.

"Let us eat and be merry!" the mayor concluded. The wine started flowing. "Musicians, play music! It's Danny's night!"

Somebody stuck a glass in Danny's hand. Adamo came up and asked, "Are you ready to party?"

"Sure. and I'm thinking about joining that group dance they are doing. It looks like fun."

"This is my girlfriend, Martina. Martina, meet Danny, "The Border Phantom." The handsome Adamo smiled at them both. Come, let's join the dancing.

The three young people danced and laughed until the music stopped, momentarily.

"I bet you are hungry. Let's go get some food. Martina, you help Danny fill up a plate, but easy on the wine. Americans are not used to drinking like we are. Don't give him too much or my father will get on to me."

"Sit at this table," Adamo said, as he pulled out a chair for Martina. "There's plenty of room for the three of us. Danny, everybody here will want to shake your hand and speak to you. Sorry, that's the price of fame." he smiled. "Just try to eat between handshakes. Don't want you to go hungry!" Adamo raised his glass and toasted, "To new friendships!" Martina and Danny clinked their glasses with his.

"Tell me, Danny, do people really call you The Border Phantom?"

"Yes, some people do, but to me it's a fun thing. I'm all right with most anything," Danny answered and laughed.

The band played fast and loud. Everybody was happy. They were glad to be able to poke the Russians in the eye for a change. And their guest, Danny, had made it possible. Many people came up to thank Danny and to shake his hand.

"Danny, was your meal good? Want some more? We have plenty spread out on the tables," Adamo offered.

"No, that was a fantastic meal. I don't think I have ever seen so much food in one place and it is all so good. What do we do now? Should we join the circle dance that's going on?"

"Absolutely, Danny. We Italians are all about fun and enjoying ourselves, and tonight is a fun night, in your honor."

Danny, Adamo, and Martina joined the festivities. People kept shoving glasses of wine in Danny's hand. Danny was afraid of drinking too much, but the night air kept trying to take over. The circle dances went around and around and then they switched direction and went round and round the other way.

After a time the band changed to slow music. The evening was coming to a close. Several young ladies danced with Danny. He felt like a rock star.

Captain Joe announced "Give me your attention, please. The night has already gone. Thank you to all my family and friends for putting on such a great reception for our young American friend, who is now an honorary citizen of our villa.

"While we were all partying I had several people come to me and ask why are we so excited about helping people we don't know? There are three good reasons. A few of you already know that during the war I was commander of a group of soldiers and caught behind enemy lines. Some of those soldiers are here with us tonight. Others will remember because it was your husband or your father with me then. These people behind the Iron Curtain helped us get around them and back to safety.

"The second reason is what the priest said, that these are real people and our Lord teaches us to love and to help. It is our Christian duty to help.

"The third reason is the one many of us appreciate the most. This act gives us a chance to get back at the Russians. We have done good work.

"So for the last time tonight I would like to propose a final toast to Danny. Please lift your glasses and toast our brave young guest."

Everybody lifted their glasses and cheered "To Danny!"

Captain Joe continued, "Now I need to get Danny to rest. Because we have an early start tomorrow. I'm going to try my best to get Danny back to Marseille tomorrow night where a ship is waiting to take him back to America. Good night and God go with you all."

The partiers slowly departed. Several came to shake Danny's hand a final time and to say good bye. Once again, Danny felt like he was home.

"Border Phantom, I'll wake you way before sunup. We'll grab our gear and go directly to my ship. We'll eat breakfast on the ship. That way we won't be as rushed while eating. Good night."

"Good night, Captain Joe. Please tell your beautiful wife that I enjoyed everything very much. Good night and thank you, my friends, Adamo and Martina." Both Adamo and Martina gave Danny brief hugs.

Danny gratefully followed the captain who showed him to his room

"Oh, such a comfortable bed," Danny thought as he lay down. Sleep overcame his thoughts in moments.

"Good morning, Danny. Ready to go? Yes, I know, it was a fast night."

Danny slowly awoke and dressed. It was going to be another eventful day. They headed down to the port where the crew had everything ready. The cook even had breakfast, and especially coffee, ready.

After eating a big breakfast Captain Joe got another cup of coffee and sat down to visit with Danny. "Today is going to be a long, tiring day. So you may as well nap when you can. We'll be just a few miles off the coast the entire time. You'll be able to see the coast but at a distance. Actually when we are underway we all get pretty bored. That is, if there are no storms to contend with. Today looks like we have clear sailing all the way.

"Now, tell me where your nick name, The Border Phantom, came from."

Danny smiled and rolled his eyes a little self consciously and explained. "Dominick, the Rom Baro in Marseille, said people wouldn't remember my name but everybody would remember and recognize a nick name. So he named me The Border Phantom, because I slipped out of the U.S. and I slipped into France, and he knew I would be slipping across the Russian border.

"But tell me, Sir, you told me there is a lot of boredom when there are no storms. And you said I have a lot of free time today. But what do you do with your free time?"

"I am working on a book, Danny. You see, when Churchill, Roosevelt, and Stalin sat down and divided up Europe at the end of World War Two they were very wrong to entrust all of Eastern Europe to the Russians. Several countries were combined to create a new country called Yugoslavia which was also given to Russia.

"While the Americans did things right by helping the countries in their sectors rebuild from all the war damage, the Russians simply took from the war torn countries in their sector. Take is all they ever do and many thousands of people have died because of them. I want to expose the Russians to the world. You will be in that book, Danny, because you have helped the resistance against the Russians.

"A book takes an incredibly long time to write and then to get it published. And that's besides all the editing and formatting. But now you go on and take a nap because you may not get a lot of sleep tonight. We have a very long day ahead of us."

Danny found his bunk. But sleep refused to come. He started thinking about the many families he had met. Every one of them had invited him back. Every one of them wanted to make Danny part of their family. "Family? I don't have a family of my own," Danny said to himself. "What is family, anyway? Just a bunch of people somewhere that you are related to. Let's see now. Who all have I met in the past few years? There was my father. Yes, he was true family. I loved and respected my father. My brothers and my mother? I never really saw much of them. My brothers were much younger. And my mother was always out shopping somewhere. I still worry what happened to my brothers after the memorial service.

"My grandparents at Rattlesnake Cove? They were good people and they loved me. Maggie Ann? I need to go back to her someday.

"The Greeks in Chicago, the Gypsies in France, the little farm house family on the Russian border, the Gypsies behind the Russian border, Captain Joe's family? All very different people. But they all had two things in common. They believed in God and they loved each other.

"I've been running from Buford but at least I've been helping other people. I think now that I have really been on a quest. A quest to find a home and a place to belong. I haven't found the right home yet, but I have learned what a home should be like. It should have God and it should have love. That is how I will work to create my future life."

The gentle waves and the big diesel engine lulled Danny to sleep. The thoughts would have to wait until another day. But Danny was on his way to creating his life plan.

"Danny, you've slept almost all day. We'll be coming into port in a couple of hours. I figured you might want to get up and eat a bite, then watch as we approach land. Your Romani friends are at the port ready to escort you to your new ride, a much bigger ship. The Baro has your bag, your flag, and everything else that was in it, as well as the money you earned in Paris. They have already converted the money to American dollars for you. They are already there waiting to see you."

Danny jumped up and went to watch as they slowly approached land. Marseille was a huge port. Danny was fascinated to see so many ships from so many countries. Captain Joe had to travel very slow and to watch for other ships in his path. It was a slow process, but exciting.

"There they are, I see them now. The Rom Baro, Dimitri, and Juliette were all three jumping up and down and waving. He's holding up my bag and Juliette is holding up my flag. I am so glad to see them."

Lines were tossed to pilings and the ships engine began idling down. A ramp was laid out and Danny ran down it to his friends.

"Welcome back to Marseille, Border Phantom," the Rom Baro said in English.

Juliette grabbed her friend's arm. "Danny, we need to get you to the ship right now because the captain is holding it for you. So we must talk while we walk. Your bravery and your courage is just amazing. You are a great American. My father, and our entire camp, will always be indebted to you.

"If you can ever find it possible, we want you to come visit us some day. So let me say it again, remember, wherever we are, we will always be your home. You will always be part of our family. We pray to God that you will find your mother. Here we are now. There's the boarding ramp."

The Rom Baro handed Danny the fishing bag Danny's daddy had made years before. Then all three hugged Danny to say good bye. Juliette gave Danny a brief kiss on the cheek. Her large dark eyes glittered with tears.

Danny trudged up the ramp and then turned to wave at them once more. As he did so, he felt a shudder go through his body. He had left yet another family.

In the dark, the sea seemed to melt into the night sky; where it met the horizon was unclear. "Like what lies ahead for me. Will I ever have a home?" thought Danny.

Meanwhile...

Deep in the Bowels of Washington, D.C.

S omewhere deep in the bowels of Washington, D.C., in the Federal Triangle there is a suite of offices known only to few. There is no name on the door. The suite entrance is protected by two muscular armed guards. People come and go, all wearing expensive three-piece suits. Nobody seems to know, or care, what they do behind that thick oak door.

Knock, knock.

"Come in" calls a deep, gravely voice. What do you have?"

"Hey boss, you remember that paper I wrote recently about the future of Europe? You wanted me to tell you more."

"So tell me."

"Well, Boss, I feel that the people behind the Russian Iron Curtain will rebel some day. The so-called Russian Iron Curtain Countries will be destroyed. The people of that made up country, Yugoslavia, are all going to want their autonomy. When that happens there will be mass killings and civil wars. We need to have our own person in place to help those people, before all that begins. Somebody who can travel across the area at will.

Somebody who has a network of support. Somebody who can facilitate taking down that curtain. We need to start looking for that person and get him trained up and ready to go. We have a few short years before it happens but I think we need to start working on it now."

"I've read your paper and studied your plan. It's a good plan. What do you need?"

"I need your approval and I need the money to make it happen."

"You will have my approval in writing and you will have the money. This is the government, remember. Money is no problem. Good luck!"

Please email me and tell me what you thought of this first in a three part series of this young man and his experiences. If you would like to be notified when the next book comes out please let me know.

Please email me at carney50@mchsi.com

Thank you very much for taking your valuable time to read this book.

David R. Carney

About the Author

Davyd R. Carney retired from the U.S. Army as a Senior Non-Commissioned Officer and is also a retired banker. He spent seven years in Europe and has traveled to over thirty countries around the world. As a young teenager, while a Boy Scout, he became very familiar with the Arizona desert.

Carney says this is not a bio, although he was able to draw on his rich background of diverse international experiences to write this story. Raised in a dysfunctional family and living in many homes across the nation while attending many schools he became a high school dropout who later earned a MBA from the University of Alabama in Huntsville. Carney well understands the plight of many young people who may be searching for a home.

Carney has been very instrumental in the military veterans community, often speaking at events as well as organizing events for deployed service members and their families. He has been recognized by the U.S. Army and also by his community for his many military and veteran activities.

He lives in the small town of New Market, Alabama with his wife, Judith, and their two cats. Judith is also a published author. They are very active in their church.

The Quest

The Quest

The Quest

Made in the USA
Columbia, SC
20 June 2019